Han Suyin was born in Pe[...] Chinese father and Belgian [...] much of her life travelling [...] West. After qualifying as a doctor at [...] University, she went to live in Hong Kong where she wrote her bestselling novel, *A Many-Splendoured Thing*, which tells her own story. She is the author of over thirty books, including four volumes on modern China which are used in universities throughout the world as essential source material on China, a two-part biography of Mao Tsetung (Dzedong) and the powerful and beautiful *Winter Love*, first published in 1952.

Alison Hennegan, the series editor of Lesbian Landmarks, read English at Girton College, Cambridge. From 1977 until its closure in 1983 she was Literary Editor and Assistant Features Editor at *Gay News*. She went on to become Editor of The Women's Press Bookclub 1984–1991 and in 1992 launched the specialist feminist Open Letters Bookclub, which she currently edits.

LESBIAN LANDMARKS

Lesbian writing is booming today – from the most rigorous of scholarly studies to the softest of soft-centre fiction – with special lesbian sections in many bookshops, crammed with volumes from the tiniest lesbian presses and the biggest publishing giants. In the midst of such plenty, it's easy to forget that it was not always so . . . .

Lesbian Landmarks is an exciting new series of reprints which illuminates the rich and eventful history of lesbian writing.

Their politics as varied as their prose and poetry, their ideas on gender as diverse as the genres in which they express them, the writers reprinted here span centuries, castes and cultures. Some were celebrated in their lifetimes but are now forgotten; others were silenced and exiled.

Amongst these authors you will find remarkable innovators in style and content. You may also find women whose far-distant attitudes and assumptions perplex or even anger you. But all of them, in their different ways, engaged in the long struggle to articulate and explore ways of living and loving that have, over the centuries, been variously misrepresented, feared, pathologized and outlawed.

The world these authors knew was often a world apart from ours; yet however unlikely it may sometimes seem, each of these books has helped to make possible today's frequently very different, confidently open lesbian writing. These, in short, are Lesbian Landmarks.

Han
Suyin

Winter Love

Introduction by Alison Hennegan

Published by VIRAGO PRESS Limited, March 1994
42–43 Gloucester Crescent, London NW1 7PD

First published in Great Britain in one volume with
Cast But One Shadow by Jonathan Cape Ltd 1962

Printed and bound in Great Britain by
Cox & Wyman Ltd, Reading, Berks.

Introduction

Isobel came to see me, and I told her my side. I said that one of the main things I could no longer stand was having to lie to everyone: for I was a Eurasian, and not pure Chinese, and Pao [her husband] had made this into a shameful thing, and I could no longer live this lie. And Isobel thoughtfully said: 'But you mustn't say Eurasian, dear, it's not a nice word.' 'But I am,' I protested, 'I must say it, I am.'

That Isobel should say this, that the very word was something to be ashamed of, so strong were the feelings of caste and the racism inherent in the British upper class, I was always to remember, especially since Isobel herself was completely free from any racialism. Never was there a woman more aware of the evils of it, more strong to combat it: but she was soberly appraising me of a fact, of a prejudice that existed.

Birdless Summer, Han Suyin

Thus Han Suyin, writing in 1968, recalls an exchange she had in 1942. Stationed in London for three years with Pao, her military attaché Chinese husband, she had finally revolted against his constant verbal insults (often public) and physical assaults. Gratefully she had taken refuge in the house of Margery Fry. An enraged Pao had blustered and blandished; had threatened to bring a legal action against her hostess whom he accused, wrongfully, of abducting his wife in a fit of lesbian passion (an emotion of which Han Suyin knew nothing at that time). When all else failed he sent friends to plead his cause with his errant wife. It was to one of those friends, Isobel Cripps, wife of Sir Stafford and president of the Aid to China Fund, that Han Suyin expressed her hatred of the lie Pao had forced her to live, and declared that she would do so no longer.

Isobel's response – 'But you mustn't say Eurasian, dear, it's not a nice word' – is shockingly vivid evidence of the power of language, and of names in particular. Scarcely a new lesson for Han Suyin: she had already seen with abhorrence how names and categories were used as vicious political weapons in her own native China, under Chiang Kaishek, and in the Hitlerian smart-set of her mother's native Belgium. Words used as weapons in the domestic sphere were, of course, all too sickeningly familiar.

A few months after that conversation with Isobel Cripps, Han Suyin resumed the medical studies she had interrupted in 1938 and became a student of the Hunter Street School of Medicine for Women. The school would furnish her with her first awareness of the possibilities of sexual love between women, and aspects of the institution itself would provide the setting for her 1962 novel *Winter Love*, which has as one of its main themes the overriding importance of naming correctly and the corrosive results of living out your lies. The volatile emotions at work in an all-female college, the bulk of whose students are still close to their mainly genteel schooldays, may seem ludicrously removed from the brutalities perpetrated by the blueshirts and brownshirts of fascist China and Germany. But part of Han Suyin's purpose is to suggest the connections between the cruelties and betrayals of private life and the larger horrors of world conflicts.

So many things could be done, and if one didn't talk about them, didn't think about them, one could live with them, they would be quite all right. But when put in words, they came barging into one's consciousness at all times, and one knew the foulness of deeds. So the important thing was not to call things by their name.

Twenty-year-old Red, a student at Horsham College of Science, in London, during the last year of the Second World War, formulates those words – but does not utter them – during one of many searching and unsettling conversations with Mara, a fellow student who is not yet Red's lover but will very soon become so. There is a word that's always threatening to barge into Red's consciousness and it's the one that she's most anxious to leave unspoken: lesbian. She's *done* it, often, lived with it for some time now, but she does not want it named, does not want it for *her* name. Like Eurasian, 'It's not a nice word'. Mara, older than Red, married, but lacking any previous sexual feelings for women, does not know yet whether 'lesbian' is an accurate name for her; but, unlike Red, once she's sure, she will claim it and live out the logic of its meaning. It may not be a 'nice word' but if it is *her* word she must use it. *Winter Love*'s main action hinges upon the roots and consequences of this crucial difference between the two women.

It is not simple cowardice which causes Red's denial (coward though she certainly is in this and – largely *because* of this – in much else besides). Anti-lesbianism was, and is, like racialism, 'a prejudice that existed', and Mara's husband, like Han Suyin's, is quite prepared to bring a legal prosecution because of it. But Red's refusal to name goes deeper than expediency. The word 'lesbian' brings with it a host of myths, judgements and injunctions – a bewildering mishmash of popular errors and unreliable, but 'expert', opinion. Theories divorced from fact abound: 'passing phases' pass; marriage and children cure it; real lesbians are born, not made (unless a real one seduces you); real lesbians can only desire, never be desired. Folk myths such as these help to fuel and render 'safe' the endless passionate friendships and 'crushes' which make up the emotional economy of student – and sometimes staff – life at Horsham College. Everyone is doing it, but no one is 'really' doing anything.

All these myths – and more – Red knows. Her relation to them is an uneasy mixture of belief and rejection. They offer comforting certainties and hideous false choices. Confronting them, questioning them, challenging them, demands more courage, more self-acceptance than she can summon. For Red has two battles to fight: one against those general, external forces which shape her generation's conceptual world; and a second, against her own personal history, from earliest childhood made up of rejection, loss and cruelty. One of *Winter Love*'s many outstanding strengths is its brilliant analysis of the connection between those two struggles. The novel offers a magnificent study of the genesis and mechanism of what we might now call internalized self-oppression, although the book was written years before the phrase was current.

It is often assumed that lesbians have been free to enjoy a greater degree of confidence and self-acceptance than homosexual men. Lesbians, unlike gay men who were, until 1967, officially ranked as criminals by an 1885 Act of Parliament, have never been subject to hostile legislation. There was, in fact, a little remembered attempt in 1921 to include lesbians in the provisions of that Act of 1885. In the end, after much anxious, often over-heated, and frequently bewildering discussion, MPs agreed that the publicity surrounding new legislation would probably do more harm than good, giving altogether too many impressionable young girls and women their first knowledge of things which it would be so much better to keep from them.

Laws or no laws however, there was still plenty of anti-lesbian hysteria in the air during the years when the young Red was growing up. Novels were a particularly potent source of myths and miseries. Clemence Dane's first – and best-selling – 1917 novel, *Regiment of Women*, both responded to and extended one particular strand of anti-lesbian animus, commonly directed against one of the largest groups of women who had professional charge of young girls: school teachers. Outside fiction the formidable Marie Stopes – in so many ways so wrongly regarded as a champion of sexual freedom – waxed luridly melodramatic in her influential and widely circulated handbook, *Sex and the Young: A Book for Parents and Teachers* (1926):

> '. . . where the staff are all unmarried I fear I am not pessimistic in saying there is increasingly the risk that there may be one or other member whose sex manifestations are not natural, and who is partly or completely homo-sexual. Such a one may have a social conscience well enough developed to restrict the expressions of abnormal feeling to an adult partner, but, on the other hand, it is not unknown (although it is generally completely hushed up) that such an individual may corrupt young pupils under his or her charge . . . . Such perverts are not so rare as normal wholesome people would like to believe . . . . Every head teacher should be eternally watchful to see that no such member is on the staff. This abnormality is extremely difficult to detect, because very often the relation with the

younger pupils is built up within a protective tissue of
romance and pseudo-chivalry which is exactly of the type
calculated to enlist every loyalty on the part of the pupil and
to keep the relation absolutely secret.'

That is truly the stuff of nightmare, its seemingly measured
style and pseudo-scientific vocabulary calmly turning other
people's virtues – protectiveness and chivalry – into tawdry
travesties for which they stand condemned. Quotations such
as that one bear out the claims of recent historians that the
semi-official campaign against unmarried woman teachers
which surfaced in the inter-war years was rooted in a growing
fear of lesbianism.

The publication in 1928 of Radclyffe Hall's *The Well of
Loneliness* (a novel which it is unfashionable to defend or
enjoy, although I do both), and the criminal prosecution
brought against its author, increased public awareness of
lesbianism's existence without necessarily effecting any
greater understanding or acceptance. Novels which treated
lesbianism as the subject of comedy (as Compton Mackenzie's
far from unsympathetic *Extraordinary Women* did), or which
softened the impact of its presence by embedding it in a work
as teasingly ambiguous and elusive as Virginia Woolf's
Orlando, escaped the law. Both those two novels were
published in the same year as *The Well of Loneliness*, but Hall's
greater directness and clear polemical intention led to her
work's suppression until after the Second World War.
(Young women such as Red may still have managed to see
one of the copies illegally, but fairly regularly, smuggled in
from Paris.)

'Lesbian' novels by hostile authors abounded in the
Thirties, many of them gaining wide review coverage, selling
well and staying in print. Novels such as these the young Red

could easily have encountered in her teens: Naomi Royde-Smith's particularly unpleasant offering for 1925, for instance, *The Tortoise-shell Cat*. And then there were books in which attitudes to lesbianism weren't uncomplicatedly hostile but nevertheless left an unsettling sense of lack, loss and confusion: Rosamond Lehmann's much celebrated first novel, *Dusty Answer* (1927), for example, or Djuna Barnes's altogether more 'high-brow' *Nightwood* (1936). And earlier novels, such as Dane's *Regiment of Women*, and its equally excitable 1918 successor, *Legend*, remained in print through the decades. With help like that, no wonder Red, and many other lesbians of the time, found it so difficult to come to terms with their love and desire for women.

Red both craves love and dreads it. She yearns for intimacy and fears the vulnerability it brings. Love terrifies her because of the dependency it entails and because all of her life, before Mara, taught her that love will be abused and exploited. Fearful of the pain she assumes will come, she seeks to inflict it first. Love and loss, cruelty and desire long ago fused for her as they did for Karl, Mara's husband (and for Pao, Han Suyin's). Male and female, homo- and heterosexual are here linked in a common pattern, and one which, Han Suyin suggests, finds its echo in war:

> We went to the pictures sometimes. War pictures,
> filled with the shriek and rent of airplane engines,
> and the bark and boom of guns. There was a
> particular one in which at a certain moment an
> English Commando bayoneted a German soldier.
> The blade went in with a sound, and a lot of people
> in the audience heaved a sigh, somewhere between
> feeling sick and pleasure . . .

Confusions of that sort have long been commonplace in Red's experience of sexual passion. Predictably, Red the emotionally abused has become Red the abuser, whilst blaming passionately those whom she abuses. Oblivious to the irony, Red's narrative offers us a life-story conceived largely as an indictment of others – including even, at the end, Mara herself:

> And Mara was wrong: she should not have
> accepted so tamely, have bowed down to my will,
> or whatever it was that made me do what I did.

'Or whatever it was . . . .' Such evasiveness is typical of Red's language throughout. At every point where a moment's searching introspection might yield painful but valuable insight into her own moods and motives, she takes refuge in conveniently nebulous phrases which obscure her own agency in the emotional history she laments. So, too, her judgements and versions of events are not to be automatically taken on trust. Her vested interests are considerable. She struggles valiantly for truth in her narrative, but some truths are too hard to face (her neurotic meanness over money, for example, which she calls 'practicality' – a virtue, in contrast to Mara's 'carelessness' in financial matters, which others might call courage or generosity). Han Suyin shows quite remarkable skill in making sure *we* know the truth, even when Red denies it still.

Many of the book's original reviewers revealed a startling lack of skill in their failure to recognize the psychological subtlety of its characterizations. Some were quite simply disgusted ('the tawdry recital of a London lesbian, of how she got that way and of what finally provoked her into marrying. Neither the cast nor the process is inviting.' *Atlantic Monthly*).

Others, anxious to display their worldly knowledge, proudly aired their grasp of lesbian slang and confidently described Red and Mara as a typical butch and femme, entirely overlooking the fact that Red realizes Mara has freed her from the constraints of a 'spurious masculinity' and has demonstrated to her, in love-making, that she is herself desirable. Most mysteriously of all, the *New York Times* reviewer, a Mrs Saal, incomprehensibly maintained that the characters 'are devoid of conflict within themselves and without. They meet, love, part – without complication or motivation.'

Winter Love is not a book to be read quickly or carelessly: clearly many of its first reviewers did both. In their haste – or ignorance – they failed to see how far removed its characters are from the period's familiar stereotypes of doomed, 'vampiric' lesbian lovers. Mara's gentleness seems to have blinded them to the formidable strength from which it grows. They possibly did not wish to share Han Suyin's own clear vision of the economic and social constraints which propel so many women into loveless and passionless marriages, undertaken only for a spurious safety and precarious status. Even less did they wish to acknowledge with her that 'small' private cruelties and mass barbarism share common roots. And they most certainly didn't want to admit that any of all this was a fitting subject for humour or tenderness, although the book offers both abundantly.

More than thirty years later, a new generation of readers should be better able to recognize and applaud Han Suyin's outstanding achievement in this, her finest novel.

Alison Hennegan, Cambridge, 1993

IT was nine in the morning, on the centre courtyard at the Horsham Science College. I was a second-year student. September 20th, 1944. London September, young, not stark cold, but flabby, shiver-making, viscous, yellow-grey chill sticking to the stones and pillars of the courtyard. All the girls were there, our year and the third year, and the new first-years huddling together embarrassed and dumb. High-voiced, self-consciously laughing groups reformed, much the same twosomes as last year moving about together again. It was a duffel-coat and macintosh year; everyone seemed to wear one. I can't see any other colour about except Mara's. To me she glowed in green and blue tweeds, standing all by herself on high heels, while colourless fawn-greys eddied round.

'Hallo, Red. Had a nice vac?'

'Yes, thanks.'

It was Louise, blue eyes looking at me, fawn camel coat. I'd protected her in First; we'd gone around together. She'd spent the short summer vac in Ireland with her people, and we'd written to each other quite a lot.

'I've bagged the best locker, Red. Came early and got it from the Frump. Told her I'd share it with you.'

'That's fine.' I stared at Mara's heels, with the nylon stockings above them. Nylons I hadn't seen except in magazines. Strictly black-market in 1944.

Louise followed my eyes. 'Who's the new bod?'

'Don't know.'

I

'Good gracious, just *look* at those nails.'

Pink varnish. Her toes might have pink varnish on, too. Her feet must be beautiful in their smooth suède navy shoes. She had black hair, longish, smooth as a blackbird's wing but the ends tipped upwards.

'Italian or French,' said Louise. 'Oh, lord, one of those married bods again. She's got a ring.'

On her left-hand ring-finger was a plain band, which I thought silver.

'It's the war,' said Louise. 'Married bods everywhere these days. Platinum ring. Bod with dough. Dog with bough.' Louise tried to talk as I did, to please. And I talked the way I did because it rather showed up the snooty ones, like Louise. I'd picked up the lingo from Rhoda, and lots of girls now thought it smart.

Daphne came up to me. 'Hallo, Red, had a good vac? You look spiffing, darling. Who's the new item?'

'Lenora Stanton Number Two,' said Louise. 'Another of those married students. What's the Horsham coming to?'

'I say, Red, will you dissect with me,' said Daphne, 'you and Louise, I mean?'

Louise looked stony and said, 'Thanks for nothing, Duffer.'

There I stood with Daphne Meredith and Louise Wells, my chums. I'd known them both since school-days, and Louise said she was in love with me. But I walked away and stood by Mara, only of course I didn't know her name. She turned her head, her forehead came up to my mouth. She had a pointed, cat's face, dark eyes, pale skin. 'I say,' I said. 'Good morning. This your first day?'

'Yes, but I'm going straight into second year. Miss Eggleston said I could.' Eggie was our Zoology Demonstrations teacher.

'Got a partner? To dissect with, I mean?'

She shook her head.

'In that case, would you like to dissect with me? I mean, if you don't mind?'

She said: 'I'd like to, of course.'

'I'll see you in the lab then,' I said. 'We're meeting there to share the bods; I mean, you know, the specimens. By the way, my name's Bettina Jones, but everybody calls me Red.... My hair' – I pointed – 'true mouse, hence Red.'

She laughed. She looked at me. I had my leather jacket on and my grey flannel skirt. I hid my hands in my pockets.

'And my name is Mara Daniels. I'll see you, Red, in the lab, as you say.'

I went back, whistling under my breath, to where Louise and Daphne stood. Louise gave me that widening of her eyelids at the outer corner of her eyes, pupils dilating then narrowing suddenly, a trick that someone, not I, must have told her made her eyes more seductive. She did that quite often. At first it had attracted me, now I suddenly didn't like it any more.

'Who's *she*?' Her lower lip tried to snake up at the word 'she'.

'Nice kid,' I said. 'I've asked her to dissect with us.'

'You've asked her ... Another Stanton married bod? You're slipping, Red. Never knew you fall for that kind before.'

Daphne just looked far-away.

'I suppose,' Louise went on, 'she'll be sharing your locker next, the one I got for us?'

'Hadn't thought of that. But I suppose I'd better get cracking finding one for her,' I said.

'Wow,' said Daphne, 'we've all had it, chum.' She stepped smartly away, her face quivering a bit.

Louise could blaze up, but she wouldn't start a scene now. She had dignity. Next thing, she was chatting and laughing with a group; that was her way of getting even with me, but I didn't care any more, and I didn't say anything as she turned her back to me.

I watched Mara. She stood against a pillar. Girls looked at her, furtively, curiously. She was going straight into second year. My year. She was to dissect with me. She stood there, not looking at anyone, not even me, a far-away composure upon her face. I knew it was the most beautiful face I had ever seen.

*   *   *

The Zoology Lab at the Horsham was as dismal as the rest of its mid 'twenties four-storeyed structure, though more recently built and full of glass windows. Just before the war some dear old Horsham girl, bursting with zeal for female emancipation, had left enough money to modernize that bit of the College. As she put it in her will: recalling the awful hours she had spent trying to get herself an education, she wanted us to be more comfortable than she'd been. Some crumbling walls had been replaced. All one end and right down one side we had plate glass staring at the sky and the serried thousands of chimney-pots of London. In 1944 with those buzz-bombs it didn't make one feel too happy. Nothing had happened as yet – the blitz had spared us – but one did feel unprotected when the V1s droned overhead.

Our cement post-mortem table, upon which lay the formalin-injected animals (we'd graduated to vertebrates and were doing cat), was in the left-hand corner, just where the glass ceiling began; and looking up from the specimens stretched out, dripping congealed grease and spreading acid chemical stench in the cold lab air, I could see a grey balloon, behind it another, and yet others, quite a lot of watching balloons, suspended in the still, grey sky.

Mara and I worked on one half of the cat. Louise with Daphne did the other half. The formalin made our eyes water, the smell made us cough. Coughing was not liked by Miss Eggleston.

'Now, now, ladies.' She would come in, tapping upon the slabs the thin wand she kept in her hand and with which she pointed at organs and exposed nerves and tendons, like a maestro at the Proms picking out the musicians with his baton. She went tap-tapping, tut-tutting, from slab to slab. Some of us she liked, others she didn't, and she never bothered to hide her feelings.

At first Eggie disliked Mara, and it wasn't difficult to know why. Mara was so different; first there were her looks, her clothes, the way she spoke. Then, about a week after we had begun on the cat, Mara went skipping down the lab to the cloakroom. Why she skipped instead of just walking I wouldn't know. She was like that at times, like a child who'd never grow up. The next day Eggie wrote in red chalk on the blackboard: 'Ladies will *walk quietly* and refrain from skipping through the Zoology Laboratories.'

Mara could not understand why, and said so.

Louise, scalpel scratching, said: 'I agree with Eggie. It's bad form, skipping.'

'Disrespect to the cats,' I explained. 'We may be cutting them up, but we've still got to show respect or something. I mean not laugh or sing or talk too loud, and all that.'

In those early days Eggie quivered with suppressed irritation whenever she saw Mara: the varnished nails, the make-up, the nylons and the heels; the over-long hair with a sheen on it. Everything about Mara meant money, care, glamour, and I suppose it offended Eggie's puritan delight in ugliness. Mara had an absent-minded, far-away ease, which often looked like impudence when it was only detachment; she didn't care what she said or did, and Eggie wasn't used to that. Most of us played up a bit to Eggie, even Lenora Stanton.

5

Mara's looks did things to Eggie; that was obvious. A lot of us during the war rather wallowed in frowziness, didn't keep our nails or hair too clean; things were hard to come by, and somehow it was good to let oneself go. Just as it was good to talk lower-middle-class talk, it made one feel somehow more 'in' with everybody else, less class-feeling about, more chummy and sturdy; it reflected the 'I-can-look-after-myself' feeling of some of us; it was an attitude, and we grew used to our own attitude.

Mara wasn't like Lenora Stanton, who insisted on telling everybody about her husband's demise, about her infants, encouraged the girls to think of free love and sex as a beautiful ecstasy, and shouted gaily at the canteen: 'What all of you need is a *man*!' when men were so damned hard to meet in those days. Mara didn't talk, but it was obvious that she had another, secret life, besides this life among the dead cats in the lab with those glacial, sky-staring windows. That bandbox look suggested care, a man who looked after her, the assurance of wealth behind her, and yet there was something slightly off key. One couldn't imagine her *not* having everything she wanted, in spite of the war. But then why was she here? Of course Eggie disapproved. The lab was Eggie's life. She was bound to it. For her, I thought, there couldn't be much else. Year after year after year she'd go on teaching zoology. We knew only that part of Eggie's life which existed in bleak day. We knew that with winter coming Eggie's nose got redder and redder, the only bright thing about her. Beyond the lab we knew nothing of her, could not imagine anything exciting happening to her. One could not visualize her doing anything other than tapping her stick and asking for the name of a bone or the comparative phylogeny of the jaw. Whereas Mara suggested ... oh, so many many things, envy-making things: warm beaches and cosmetics and music, and lots of clothes and no coupons, and eggs and tins from America, and

6

French wines, and oh, so many things we were forgetting in the war or had never had.

After I knew Mara I began to wonder about other people. I mean, about what they really were inside. Far more than I'd ever done. It was Mara who brought these thoughts to me. At the Horsham she was for ever saying and doing the wrong things, or so it seemed; always someone or other there was speculating about her, talking about this or that she'd said or done. But they kept quiet if they noticed I was about. But it didn't matter to me: I was already in love with her. I didn't like it when people said things. And as for Eggie's dislike, well, that hurt me too, but somehow it made me see Eggie differently, made her more human. I knew why she disliked Mara. But Mara's worst enemy was Louise, who made remarks whenever she could. Louise hated Mara, and I think it wasn't so much because of *me* as because Mara was so beautiful.

Because we were all girls together it was cosy, even with the malice. I mean, we felt at ease, shouting gaily to our partners after lab, striding away by twos, semi-permanent duos formed quickly or slowly, sometimes (though rarely) changed after a few months, every change bringing with it a 'situation', quarrels or tight-lipped scenes which we all pretended weren't. I'd had my situations, so far, outside the Horsham. Some of these friendships went on for years, on through life, complete and whole in themselves, requiring no one else; but they were few. The names of these became to us semi-legendary, perpetuated by generations of Horsham girls. Many more broke up. When they broke up because of another girl there was drama, or farce, or both together, but things all settled back. Sometimes a man came in and broke it up, and then we all felt it much more. And occasionally there was a tragedy, but not often at the Horsham.

Few of the girls there were permanently like that. Most of us

7

knew we'd grow out of it one day, get married as soon as we'd left, have kids. With the war we also had married women like Lenora Stanton, who took a course in science in order to do war work later, or so she said. Lenora was a Pain, and I did my best to avoid her. I disliked her on sight. But she had her own little court, girls who hung on her lips and went round talking of Life as it ought to be lived, as a Grand, Glorious Experience, and of Woman's Role, and the Love-Life. Lenora had been an actress for a short while; her actor husband had died trying to vacuum the carpet. 'Electrocuted,' she Tallulah'd in ringing, stage tones, 'he was electrocuted. I came home to find him dead, holding the vacuum cleaner.' No one in her coterie seemed to think it funny.

Lenora was now getting married again, and hinted she would soon be doing a hush-hush war job with her new husband. Meanwhile she wanted all of us girls to understand Life and Love, and we were spared nothing of her grand, glorious clinches with her husband-to-be. Lenora had travelled a bit, and after the war she and her husband intended to settle down in Australia. He was part-Australian, which she didn't seem to mind at all, though it made Louise snigger: 'The great wide open spaces.'

'Of course,' Lenora used to scream gaily, 'they're *terribly* conventional over there. I mean, at parties all the women sit together and all the men sit together, and they never *talk* to each other. And if a girl crosses over to talk to the men, all the other women gang up against her and say she's *Fast*.' Her eyes shone happily; she was looking forward to preaching the Love-Life in Australia.

Lenora, in that same ringing voice, told me one day about Eggie. It seems that she'd gone to tea with Eggie once, for, incredibly enough, Eggie *liked* Lenora Stanton. 'Lives with her friend in a small flat down the Bayswater Road. Friend's a biologist, female of course. Poky little place, lace curtains, fringed lampshades, crochet rugs and all that sort of thing, and of course a tom-cat ... neutered,' she added.

Apart from Lenora and Mara, the married ones in our year, our landscape was female, spinster: young, eager and boisterous, or greying, middle-aged and abrupt. The young men were away at war, and many of us had come up from school without meeting them as we ought to have done. There were lots of Eggies everywhere doing wonderful work, aftermath of the First World War.

To begin with, Mara looked like a hopeless student. How they ever took her straight into second year I couldn't guess. How they ever took her anyway I never knew. They must have had a vacancy, and she got it. At the first three quizzes, whenever Eggie asked a question she did not even try to answer, but said: 'I don't know,' and Eggie kept on at her.

'That's not good enough, Mrs Daniels. I *know* you may have many other more interesting avocations, but we take our work seriously here.'

'Yes,' said Mara. And looked remote, away.

I sat with my hands in my pockets. I couldn't do anything – not even talk about it afterwards with Mara. I was ashamed for her, and unhappy that she made such a poor show. But she would smile at me as if it was nothing at all. Now I know it wasn't, but then I was still at school and I had the reflexes of a schoolgirl. I wanted her to be brilliant and popular, to protect her and shield her from Eggie, shield her from the taunts of the other girls, especially from Louise with all the answers. Everybody knew that Louise would get a Distinction. She always got top marks, always worked hard filling notebook after notebook with that even, smooth writing of hers, and now when Mara said, 'I don't know,' Louise sniggered and Eggie tapped her wand to bring back order.

'Don't think our friend will linger with us very long,' said Louise airily one lunch-time as I waited for Mara in the canteen. Mara and I had 'our' seats in the lecture room, 'our' table in the canteen.

'None of your business,' I replied.

'Of course not, Red, my poppet,' said Louise delicately. 'Let nature take its course. She shouldn't have come to the Horsham. She should hang on to whatever man she's got hold of and stay at home. She's only keeping someone else out of a career by coming here.'

I didn't reply, and then Mara arrived, and after lunch we went for a walk in the park. There was going to be a mid-term quiz in a week. I felt unhappy about it, and I said, 'Look, Mara, I've got some notes. They're not much, but you won't have to plough through the whole book. Think it might help?'

'Oh, thank you,' she said, 'but I enjoy reading zoology.'

'Look here,' I said, 'you're supposed to know your bit, especially the mammal you're dissecting I mean, otherwise Eggie won't let you go on. I mean, it's quite stiff, the competition.'

'Too bad,' said Mara.

We went in St James's Park, but it was dark when we got there and so I walked home with her. She lived in Maybury Street. We'd been dissecting four weeks. A week ago I had walked home with her for the first time. She had turned at the corner and said, 'Good night, Red.' I knew she didn't want me where she lived. And I didn't want her to know where I lived, because I was afraid she'd find it too dingy. I could picture her going back to a beautiful place – glamorous, warm, exciting – with rugs and satin-smooth curtains, not at all like Eggie's poky flat, not at all like my bed-sit in Camden Town with the dining room in the basement, the smell of frying everywhere, the cat's hair in the tea, and Andy and his pals – the medical students from

St Thomas's – smelling of formalin as I did after a dissection (only they didn't seem to wash), and sweat and dirty clothes. And Nancy, who ran the boarding-house, with her blonde dyed hair, and her boy-friend Edward, the travelling salesman who did Swedish exercises in the bathroom, and her dentures she left lying about, and the stomach ulcers which gave her halitosis ...

I went home and prayed hard that Mara would get through the first quiz, and me too, of course, but I didn't believe she could do it. I'd never worried over anyone else getting through quiz before.

* * *

'Well,' I kept on saying, 'well, well.'

We walked along the Embankment. I heard Mara's footsteps and mine sounding together, and those of a bobby on his beat ahead of us. There seemed no other sound on that Sunday afternoon: a cold and silent river, a languid flow of hours about us. London was all beautiful pictures, grey and silver: delicate airy buildings traced against silver sky, the balloons anchored puffs swaying in a sprightly wind. Even the sunlight was silvery. Mara's footsteps tuned with mine; her heels tapped the stones, my flat soles an accompaniment to their neat tap. I can still hear us and the bobby, and me saying, 'Well, well.'

'Well, well,' she parodied, laughing at me.

'Mara,' I repeated, 'you've done it.'

I'd said it at least ten times, elated by her triumph as if it were mine. I went over it again. I kept on thinking of it, thrusting my hands in the pockets of my macintosh, breathing in the cold air. It was wonderful walking on a Sunday afternoon on the Embankment with Mara, recalling the way Eggie had sat at the head of a long, narrow table, we girls grouped round bones, and bits of formalin-soaked cat, fish, frog, scattered around. Eggie held the bits up, or pointed at them with her wand, precise, ironical if one didn't know, full of impatient knowledge which made us stammer and become unsure. Her eyes darted from girl to girl, her stick pointed. This was the test which I thought Mara would fail.

Louise had asked her as we settled for the practical test: 'Do you know any zoology, Mrs D.?'

'Do you?' Mara had countered.

Louise had tinkled a laugh, amused, superior.

When it came to Mara's turn everyone, it seemed to me, leaned towards her in cruel, glittering expectancy of error. But Mara knew. The stick went from piece to piece, prodding, insisting, and the answers came easily, so pat that at one point she seemed to be ahead of the question, to harry Eggie on. It was a wonderful show. Even Louise couldn't have done better. And then Eggie, rigid yet game, said, 'Congratulations, Mrs Daniels.'

There was a cold silence as Eggie walked away, and then I began whistling. I always whistle when I'm happy.

One or two girls came up to Mara and said, 'Good show,' and 'I say, you *have* kept your light under a bushel.'

'Well, well,' I said, 'you're a dark horse, Mara.'

'Oh no,' said Mara, 'I just learned it up quickly.'

'After this,' I said, 'I'll be asking *you* to coach me. If you're as good in physiology and organic, I'll be taking lessons from you.'

We leaned over the parapet on the Embankment and looked at the muscular river silently swinging its brown barges. I still remember upon her face that day the reflected sheen of water, light from sky into river and back into her face. Thus with my happiness; it came from her, through her achieved, made whole.

We had tea in a sweaty, smoky little café, where taxi-men and the like ate fish and chips, a roaring, smoky throng of men, alien to us, altogether cut off from us. Then I saw her home to Maybury Street in Mayfair, stood with her at the corner; she walked back with me to Oxford Circus; I walked back with her. I could not bear to leave her. For ever, it seemed, we would be walking enchanted, untiring, back and forth, footsteps together in the cold night streets.

*　*　*

Each morning now, getting up earlier by half an hour than before I knew her, I gulped breakfast, hurried to catch the trolley, then changed buses twice to get to the corner of her street, there to wait for her. Every morning recurred the anxiety that I might be late, that she might have been waiting and, not seeing me, gone ahead, and I wouldn't know whether she'd gone or not and I would wait and be late at the Horsham. But it did not happen. Always I was there first, and after a short while saw her come walking down the street towards me.

It was a very cold November. I heard myself saying it as I stamped my feet, as we caught our bus to the Horsham. But I did not mind it as much as I had always minded winter, for I'm a naturally cold person; the doctor told me my circulation was poor, and I get chilblains. But this winter there was an eagerness in me which made me forget the painful smart of my customary chilblains, the frowstiness of Nancy's bed-sit. Perhaps because I spent shillings more carelessly, keeping the gas-fire on, sitting for hours in front of it, dreaming.

In the afternoon I walked with Mara back from the Horsham. Sometimes we'd stop for tea at an A.B.C., and then suddenly she would say: 'Oh, it's late, I must get back,' with a little anxiety in her voice. Off we would go then, and yet, in spite of her saying how late she would be, we would linger at the corner of her street. It was so dark with the blackout I could only guess her face as we said good night; sometimes I thought I could see it, pale, nearly luminous, like a pearl in the darkness. She would say: 'Well, Red, see you tomorrow.'

'Tomorrow. I'll be here.' I would turn and walk away. She always waited until I turned. I felt her eyes on my back.

At other times she wouldn't mind what time it was, and would walk part of the way to Camden Town with me, and I'd walk with her back to the corner of her street, Maybury Street, again. We must have tramped miles every day.

One day, at the A.B.C. where we were having tea, she said: 'Would you like to see where I live?'

I knew the house she lived in: 34 Maybury Street, it said on the register at the College. Mara Daniels. I had walked up the street early one Sunday morning (Sundays we never saw each other), hoping she might accidentally come out of the house. Number 34 was a fair-sized brick house, good-looking, rich-looking; hers the flat on the third floor, the name was under the bell-button. She must be very well-off, living in such a place: expensive flats, a good address.

When Mara said: 'Would you like to?' I was happy, yet frightened. We walked up Maybury Street, meeting two pros, scarcely in ambush yet, still slacking, talking to each other. We entered the hallway. There was a chap in uniform in a kind of booth there, who said: 'Good evening, madam.' We walked to the lift, all polished wood, with seats of red leather. Everything smelt of polish and warmth, not nose-plugging grime and cold. The house enveloped one with a warm, tranquil, rich kind of smell, good polish and regular dusting and fires kept going.

'You do live in a posh place, Mara.'

She said: 'We've got a char who comes in twice a week, and the porter downstairs is awfully good at keeping the place warm.'

She opened the door of the flat with a Yale key; then we were inside.

'We took it furnished,' she said, shutting the door on us.

It was good furniture, and well kept. But it didn't seem to mean much to her, one way or the other. She moved about easily, but she wasn't showing it as her own.

'Want a bath?' she asked.

'Do I look dirty?'

She looked at me, my duffel-coat, my grey wool skirt. 'Oh, Red, you told me yourself your pipes had burst.'

That was true. It had been freezing and there was no water at Nancy's boarding-house. Nancy had announced it at breakfast in her disaster voice, the one she reserved for the cat's misdeeds and pregnancies, or a particularly bad bout of her gastric ulcers.

'I'd *love* a bath, chum.'

She opened a door upon the bright glaze of tiled walls; a tap turned, I heard the clink of glass, she came back. 'The water's boiling hot.'

I went into the bathroom and she shut the door on me. The bathroom was full of fragrant steam; there was a large glass jar full of bath salts, and I could see from the yellow-green tinge of the foaming water that Mara had poured some into the tub.

When I came out of the tub there was the towel, large, pink; and putting on my clothes I felt them sour-smelling, stiff with cold dirt. I had not noticed the collar of my shirt before. I didn't like my clothes one bit.

I came out. Mara was sitting on the bed. It was a big bed, or rather two beds made up as one. It had a wonderful bedspread, something beige and shining which made one think of smooth skin. I sat on it next to her. I was at ease now, a dreamy softness about me, looking at the bedspread, suddenly helpless in a sea of memories, transported back to a similar moment of childhood, not recollected until now. Like a wave it swept me up: memory of a warm night, a scent of lilac, the soft arms of my mother. She wore a satin dress, something the colour of the bedspread, her bare arms glowed. She'd smelt so nice. I had nuzzled into her dress, hard.

'Verbena,' said Mara. 'Did you like it?'

'What is?' For a moment I was confused. Was it the perfume of many years back, enclosed memory of warmth and fragrance dwelling deep within my frosted childhood, that she meant? How did she know its name?

'The bath salts, Red. You were sniffing, just now. I thought you'd like to know they're verbena. They're from Switzerland.'

I smelt the back of my hand, smiled at her. She was smiling at me.

'Oh Mara,' I said, 'it's nice to be here, with you.'

'It's nice with you, Red.'

I put out my hand, and there was hers, underneath mine. It was small, compared with mine. I was glad it was so. Glad of the silk under me. Glad. I could have fallen asleep.

'Come,' said Mara, 'I'll show you something.'

Another door, locked. She took a key from her pocket, turned it, found the light-switch. A small, bare room, an easel, canvases with colour on them, one on the easel, others turned against the wall.

'I didn't know you were an artist,' I said.

I walked up to the easel, but she pulled me back.

'Don't look,' she said. 'I do it for fun.'

'So long as you know it's just fun,' I said lightly. There were lots of bright colours. I didn't know whether it was good or not, but it was Mara, so I said: 'It's awfully nice, chum.'

'Oh, I know I'm no good,' she said.

We went back to the bedroom.

16

I heard the lock turn, knew the outside door had opened. Mara rose quickly, crossed to the living room. I followed her.

It was a man, coming in and taking off his hat, and Mara saying: 'Oh, Karl,' and to me: 'Red, this is my husband, Karl.'

I wanted to look at Karl, but first I stared at Mara because her voice had changed so much. It was different now, small and stiff. There was nothing to be scared of, but I was scared. The man stood there, rubbing his hands against each other. He wasn't tall; he had long blond hair, a little too long at the back; he was handsome, with eyes appearing hazel-green through his horn, rimmed glasses; his eyes were careful.

'Karl,' said Mara, 'this is Bettina Jones. She came to have a bath, as the pipes have burst in her digs.'

'I wish,' he said, with a slight foreign accent, 'that my wife wouldn't use these slang words, Mara.'

We shook hands, then he withdrew his hand from mine and started rubbing his hands one against the other as if soaping them. Nice, revolting hands, shapely, manicured nails. I could hear the rubbing sound as he said: 'It's on the thaw now, but I expect it'll turn cold again.'

Mara said: 'I'll make some tea,' and disappeared.

We sat in the living room, and he asked me how long I had been at the Horsham and what I intended to do after the war, and I knew Mara hadn't spoken to him about me; he hadn't known I existed until now. He kept looking at me in a careful way, all over, then his eyes dropped as if I wasn't worth looking at much, and he turned his head as if listening for Mara in the kitchen; and she came in with a tray, and then he started baiting her. Baiting is the only word for the way he spoke to her, as we drank the cups of tea Mara produced.

'How was your cat today?' he said heavily, expecting us to

giggle, I bet. And he sniffed at the air: 'I don't think pretty women should take up ill-smelling studies, like zoology,' he said. And then: 'Don't you think I'm a model husband, Miss Jones, allowing my wife to spend her days cutting up dead cats? But so long as they are dead, and she is my loving wife when I am at home ... ' And he laughed.

I stood between them, although I had only just come in on the scene and he hadn't known of me. I didn't like Mara any more while Karl was there. She was so brittle, talking on a false, high note I had not heard, trying to head him off by elaborating about my bath and that there was no water where I lived, that the pipes had burst with the frost.

'Oh dear me,' he said with a smirk, turning to me, 'why don't you choose a decent place to live in? But then it is so difficult in London, such a dirty place, London. I am longing to get back to the Continent,' he said. And talked about how badly built the houses were in England.

And I said with some heat: 'Well, we're being bombed, you know.' And then I found myself saying yes, I'd love a flat like his – Mara gave me a tortured look – and how kind Mara was, asking me to have a bath, how grateful I was to *both* of them, what a lovely flat they had, and how wonderful it must be always to have hot water, wish I'd got something like that. But I could feel my heart going thump thump all the time I spoke, as if I'd done something wrong. And Karl rubbed his hands and said he was glad that I had come, and he hoped that I would look after Mara and not let her work too hard.

'I don't understand why she wants to study zoology. She does not *need* to do any work. She has a good husband to provide for her. What can a woman who is so pretty want to study for?'

Mara said, all brittle: 'But you're so often away, and I get bored doing nothing.'

It sounded coy and silly, and I felt ashamed for her, so I heaved myself off the chair and said: 'Well, I must be toddling along.' Everything we three said was all wrong; toddling sounded as if I'd said a dirty word. 'Good night, Mara,' I said. I always added: 'See you tomorrow,' when I left her after saying good night, but this time I didn't.

And she said: 'Good night, see you at the Horsham tomorrow.'

Did that mean I wasn't to wait for her at the corner the next morning? Her eyes were wide and dark as she followed me to the door, only to shut it on me. Click, it went, and I was in the lift, going down, down, and my heart seemed to go down with it; then in the street, with the smell of the slush freezing up again, a smell drawn right into me as I took a big breath.

So, I thought, that's her husband, Mr Daniels. Karl. They lived together in that flat. I saw the big bed again, and the beautiful cover on it. They slept in it, together. Mara and that man. That awful man.

I could visualize Karl clearly as I walked back. Good-looking, blond, nice eyes, nice hands. Nice husband Mara had. Just a trace of accent; he wasn't English. Trying so hard to sound English. And brutal all the way through – I was sure he was brutal. I'd behaved like a fool, blushing and stammering. After all, what was wrong in Mara and me being friends?

Then I was back at Nancy's and going up the stairs. Andy was coming down them with his striped hospital scarf round his neck; he had bought it second-hand from his brother, now in the R.A.F. Corduroy trousers, a duffel-coat, a hospital scarf, and a small stiff moustache above it all. He was trying to copy Big Brother George.

'Sniff … um … ' He stopped. 'Where'd you get that? On the blackmarket? Smells like Fifi.'

(Fifi was, possibly, an invention of Andy's, a Free French

woman, enamoured of his virile charms. I had nevea bothered to find out.)

'Let go of me, Andy. Hands off.'

'My, aren't we high and mighty tonight? Come on, just going on a pub-crawl. Fun.' He winked.

'No, thank you.'

'Oh, come on.' He squeezed himself against me, moustache searching. 'C'mon.' He drooled a bit.

'No, no.'

'Aw, now, old thing, be a good sport, like you were last time, remember? You need it, you know.'

'You –' I said. I pushed him hard against the wall so that the back of his head hit it. He let go, astonished at my violence.

I ran up to my room, slammed the door; locked it though I knew Andy wouldn't come. I wasn't really frightened of him. A silly medical student boasting of his affairs with French girls. I'd let him, a couple times, out of curiosity and because he said, 'Aw, be a good sport,' and swore he'd be careful, and I wanted to be a good sport and broad-minded, not silly and old-fashioned. Also I wanted to know what it was like. I mean, one does want to find out what it's all about. But I hadn't felt anything, not one way or the other.

It's so strange to think back to Andy then, when he's so respectable now, a different person, getting fat, and fussy about his clothes. He's my husband and I'm used to him. We don't talk about the past. Why should we? Andy has never guessed about Mara. That's one more reason I can't love him; he'll never know how I *can* feel, *can* love ... He just hasn't a clue. And though he keeps me safe, I know I'll leave him one day, walk out of this safety which is a mess.

*   *   *

20

I expected Mara to look different the next morning. Yet why should she? Because I had seen Karl? He came home every day, didn't he? That flat was their home. That bed.

I was uneasy as I strolled in the locker-room, talking to the Frump who cleaned the lavs, waiting for Mara. There was a weight in my chest; I wanted to see Mara, her smile; I also wanted to have a fight with her, to say harsh, hurting things.

I was all clenched and raw when her perfume reached me. (Louise was always catty about Mara's perfume. It heralded her, filled the locker-room, we all sniffed it, deliberately or unconsciously. 'God, that awful *scent*,' Louise would say, tossing her hair and rolling her eyes. Even in the lab, with the throat-scratching smell of the specimens, we caught Mara's perfume. Eggie must have hated it, but it wasn't a thing she could stop by writing on the blackboard about it.)

Mara stood near, glowing as if bathed in sunlight, little gold ear-rings in her ears.

'Where you going, chum? Lunch with the Duchess again?' That was a joke of mine, when she appeared all dressed-up.

She had a thinness of gaiety laid like make-up upon her face, already that smile line at one corner of her mouth etched an ambiguous droop, joy using the same line as sorrow. And I thought this face held all I meant of happiness … until I lost it, and the loss would burn in me slowly, like a cigarette-burn spreading, sloven-sure. Oh God, to think that for years I may go on like this, wanting to see that face, till the unholy time when all things blunt, and hurt or joy are no more, when all is as if it never had been …

'Not a Duchess. Friends. Nice people for a change; we're taking them out to lunch at the Hungaria.'

We. That meant Karl. Mara's married. Got a husband. It would burst the bubble of whatever friendship Mara and I had for each other if I became obsessed with Karl. I don't like Karl, but I'm sure Mara does. It's natural that she'd be happy going out with friends and her husband. Leaving me alone during the lunch hour.

'That's fine,' I said. 'By the way, I've got a date tonight, too. Won't be able to walk home with you.'

'Oh Red, too bad,' she said. But she didn't look unhappy, and I only hurt myself.

We changed into our white coats. It hurt all over to be with her, because there was something newly inaccessible to me which I hadn't been aware of, and I wanted to break it. I wanted to be with her, not shut out, like that, by a couple of friends and lunch; by her husband, her other life, friends she would go out with, all dressed-up. She never dressed up for me. How would it look if I took her to lunch at the Hungaria? Odd, two women together.

I looked at her ear-rings, and went soft inside, soft and shaky. I wanted to put out my hand and touch them, and I had to shove my hands deep in my pockets because suddenly I also wanted to tear them off her ears. She'd cry then. I wanted to see her cry, badly.

Mara would be going out to lunch, she wouldn't sit with me at our table in the canteen, she wouldn't be back until the lecture at three that afternoon, and three o'clock was a terribly long time away.

She was cheerful. We weren't dissecting any more, but looking at slides and bones. She was far from me, and then gone.

All through lunch I hated her and Karl. Last night I had thought that she was scared of Karl, but I was damn wrong, she wasn't a bit scared. She loved him. She'd no use for me except as a convenience. He was her husband, and they lived together in that warm, expensive flat. She waited for him, and they went out to meet exciting people, and he came back and made love to her; and for him Mara put little gold ear-rings in her ears.

* * *

I sat with Louise in the lecture theatre at three that afternoon, and there was no place for Mara in our row when she came in a few minutes after Eggie had begun. Louise sniggered. She was happy to be back with me, I told her I'd walk home with her that evening. Mara saw us, I think, but her face didn't change and she walked along the steps at the side to a higher row. Eggie stopped lecturing. We could hear Mara's heels clicking up the steps.

We all stopped writing, looked at Mara walking the steps on high heels, waiting for some scathing remark from Eggie, something we could rehearse and comment on later. Faces grinned, bodies settled back. 'She'll catch it.' All of us waited for Eggie's words slung at Mara like arrows, for the blood-letting. We weren't beastly, just girls out of school; cruel only in a group, foretasting a pack relish at someone's pain, or just welcoming a relief from boredom, from the drone of Eggie's voice.

Still Eggie didn't speak, only her face got slowly more purple as she looked at Mara.

'Oh boy, now wait for it.' Louise glowed, her lips moving.

I lowered my head and pretended to read my notes. I felt beastly, yet glad too, in a way. That would teach Mara to go out with gold rings in her ears.

And still there was nothing. I had to look up again to see why there was nothing. Mara was sitting there on the top row alone, fountain-pen in hand, looking at Eggie with a reflective, nearly tender smile. Her eyes didn't leave Eggie, and Eggie was staring at her as if she were trying not to choke. Then Eggie sighed, her eyes dropped, and she went on lecturing.

23

Our pens scratched assiduously, following Eggie's voice, precise and dry. Louise's pen ran her impeccable handwriting along, she squeezed the holder a little too hard.

I couldn't do anything but wait for Mara afterwards, wait for her by our locker, acquiescent, waiting, in acknowledgment of her strength: for in all of us there is this submission to someone who has earned our respect; the way the others made room for Mara, a scarcely perceptible hush in their voices even if they pretended to be unaware of her, proclaimed it too. She was somebody now. She had beaten us all, beaten back into us the ever-present, smug, pin-prick sadism towards someone different. She was different, but she was strong, and I was proud of her, even more than after the quiz.

'May I see you home?' I said.

'What about your date?'

'It's off,' I lied.

'All right,' she said. But there was no victory in her voice. She looked tired, she had the face of a beaten child. She did not say anything about Eggie or arriving late, though later I was to find out that she'd apologized to Eggie. Somehow it wasn't surprising to me that after that Eggie began to like Mara; stopped to talk to her about zoology, always zoology, and smiled at her a rapid, quickly withdrawn smile.

* * *

The London winter deepened. It was bitterly cold all the time; and dark, the sun never there, round-the-clock glumness, dim to dark and back again. Yet this was my enthralled time, such as I had never had, such as would not recur. O halcyon winter, solstice of my days … a magic ring of hours, rounding itself within the undiscerning dark. I have stepped out of this charmed circle, gone on living, not wanting anything strongly. Should I be asked now what I wanted of life, I would say, 'Happiness, I suppose,' then add quickly: 'But I'm *quite* happy, you know. A good husband, a child ... ' If I were to tell the truth, that their existence, my family's being in my proximity, remains vague to me as tombstones of strangers in a common cemetery, that only a certain winter exists for me, vivid and clear, surging with life, and that all else is neutral, formless, indifferent, people would think me queer. Only when my mind goes back to that London winter do I feel alive, instead of merely knowing as a fact that I live. In that closed memory do I count my heartbeats by the spirited blood's surge, there once again I walk with Mara through the evening that is night, holding an electric torch in my hand, the blacked-out glass letting through a faint yellow ring at our feet, and I know what it is to love, to want to die for love. This is still so, and I'm a married woman with a child.

We talked a lot, Mara and I, at first not about us but of books, people, places, ideas ... then later of ourselves, more and more. I could talk and talk and talk, and it was like being a child again, comforted, full-fed and never tired. But I don't remember our words well, in fact I can scarcely recall one thing she said of all the things which at that time seemed so important and vivid. I remember our walking together best, the pacing, the streets, the cold, beneath invisible balloons of a haunted sky, forgetting the winter and the cold. Now it becomes in my day-dreams a walk through sunlit spaces, under windless trees, amid quiet grass. At the time our surroundings would on occasion break into our consciousness: a screech of buses, the rumble of the Underground, the tremor of the stone underfoot; hurrying passers-by, shoulders hunched, pounding with feet eager to run into tea-shops, to catch buses, away from the cold. But we were close held in mutual enchantment, and lingered on in the cold streets, pacing a lovely spring, unheeding, oblivious except by fits and starts of all that went on round us.

Of other winters I remember chiefly the unpleasantness, how ugly and painful to get up, to shiver, to catch overcrowded buses; the Underground smell of feet and breaths and rancid smoke; my hands rough with chilblains, clothes cold and stiff with grime. But about this winter, Mara's winter, I continue to feel its substance, the wrench of its happiness like a pain, an ecstasy which flares up, despite what we did to each other; even when I was trying to kill it.

Whatever has happened, there is always that magic winter haunting and hurting me with its marvellous echoes. The shortest days of the year, when nothing had begun and nothing had ended, all the roads of life were alive, and time beat round me like a heart.

I remember small, precious winter fragments, snatched out of darkness and oblivion. Mara saying to me one day as we left the Horsham: 'Do you always wear slacks or skirt and that leather jacket?' I said: 'Always in winter. Can't keep warm otherwise.' I remember the way I showed her, the first day, where to hang her coat: 'If you want to use a peg in the cloakroom, write your name on it and tell the Frump.' 'Why my name?' she asked. 'Because otherwise someone else will bag it,' I said. Our locker, I remember that locker so well, the locker Louise had found for me and which I gave to Mara to share with me. I got a good strong padlock for it, and we each had a key, Mara and I. And soon everything in the locker smelled of her perfume. One day Mara wanted to go home earlier, Karl had a party or something, and of course she'd left her own key at home. I let her have mine, and instead of bringing it back to me she went off with it. Next morning she appeared without either her key or mine, and I

26

spent a long time unscrewing the latch of the steel locker, while she stood by and alternately looked rueful or laughed as if it were very funny. I was angry and yet all the time I loved her more, and now my fingers ache with unused love as they rehearse the unscrewing, the lifting of the latch, my ears rehearse her laughter: 'Oh Red, you're so clever!'

Our first lunch at the canteen together. The hubbub of voices, beef stew, then pudding with custard. The first day of term the food was generally good. I watched her eat. I was already in love with her. Right from the first moment.

Yet at times I felt that Mara was a bad spell cast upon me, something I must break away from. I was enchanted, but also terrified. She had dominion over me, and I resented it. Writing this now, the old exaltation is back, and also the old hatred and desire to hurt. There is nothing to break away from, yet I still am not delivered of this love and hate, vampire memories of the past which suck meaning out of every hour of my existence; memory of love sharp and sweet and nothing like it ever to be. Sometimes I want to be made free of that winter; and yet, and yet, I'd give everything to see Mara again.

One afternoon out walking I said to her abruptly: 'Sometimes I feel tied to you, I feel you're dragging me behind your heels, as a puppy dragged by a lead.'

As I spoke there came along a little peke, gloriously free, with a lead trailing behind its flag of a tail. We both dissolved in laughter. 'Red,' she said, 'I'm not dragging you. Perhaps you're dragging me, but I don't mind.'

We went to the pictures sometimes. War pictures, filled with the shriek and rent of airplane engines and the bark and boom of guns. There was a particular one in which at a certain moment an English Commando bayoneted a German soldier. The blade went in with a sound, and a lot of people in the audience heaved a sigh, something between feeling sick and pleasure, and Mara got up and left.

'I can't stand it,' she said, 'it's beastly.'

'But Mara, you know we've got to fight this war. It's the Germans who are beastly. Hitler's a monster.'

'I know,' she said, 'but I still don't like it. All this killing, it's insane. There's no need of war. Or if there must be, let the politicians go and fight duels, it would be cleaner.'

It sounded childish and awfully romantic, and a bit unpatriotic, but even that didn't matter. Mara was different.

One day I asked Mara what I had wanted to ask her for a long time. 'Mara, why isn't your husband fighting? Is he a V.I.P. or something?'

'Karl? Oh, he's ... ' Her voice flattened. 'Karl's got a Swiss passport. He's neutral.' And then she added: 'Don't let's talk about him.'

But I persisted, to wrest from her something about herself and Karl. 'Well, all I can say is, you're lucky having your husband with you these days.'

'Oh, Karl isn't always here,' she said. 'Besides, I don't like men.'

That day I felt much happier, freer, as at a boundary crossed. I wasn't afraid of Karl any more. Mara didn't really like him. I wanted to sit in the flat and look him over carefully, as he had looked at me. I wouldn't be shy and stutter this time. Mara said she didn't like men. That included Karl. But if she didn't, why had she married him?

I did see Karl again. About a fortnight after that first time Mara suggested my coming again to her flat. I said: 'No, don't bother,' but of course I wanted to come. But then Daphne also came with us, and had a bath. Mara had heard her complaining of the pipes at the place where she lived, and had asked her too.

28

'You're awfully awfully generous,' I told Mara. I was cross because Daphne was with us, I didn't want her. I was angry with Mara for asking her too, so casually. But lots of the girls now liked Mara. Daphne positively grovelled in front of her, though she was cautious not to monopolize her and ask her out or make a bid for her, she knew how I would react.

After baths we sat in the comfortable living room, and had coffee and hot buttered toast, and that was the second time I saw Karl. He came in, just as Daphne was going through one of her interminable stories about her aunt, who was a *terror* as well as a *character*. Karl displayed excellent manners. Again he tried to say all the right things but they sounded all wrong, though Daphne giggled and said: 'Oh, Mr Daniels!' He poured some brown sherry for Daphne, saying her eyes were brown like the sherry. Daphne looked up at him adoringly, and I thought they looked like a cow's. After that Daphne adored Karl as well as Mara, spoke of them as such a lovely, intellectual couple. Daphne is now in Africa, running a school.

Some time after, Mara said: 'Coming home with me?' and I followed her. Karl was already there, and I thought Mara didn't expect him. She was stiff, a strained smile pinned on to her mouth, eyes looking nowhere, not at me. Karl made awful conversation, about books and art and music. He showed me that I didn't know much, and then rubbed his hands together and looked at Mara and made a joke about her studying zoology: 'I think she'd like to cut *me* up too, like a frog.' It went on and on, and I knew he did not want me there, he wanted to be alone with Mara, but I also knew she did not want me to leave. And I did not want to go, I wanted to stay on being with Mara, just to annoy him ...

Finally there was a silence, and he said: 'It is getting late, shall I see you home?' Which was rude of him.

And so I said, starting as if I was surprised: 'Goodness, I

hadn't realized it was so late. I must toddle off.' This time Karl saw me to the door, down the lift. In the lift he didn't speak to me, kept looking at the floor. Then he said: 'Good night,' shook hands, the lift gate clanked shut, and I heard him open the door of his – their – flat, then slam it.

And I felt unwanted, shut out. Jealousy like a clamp round me, an intercostal jabbing hurt, squeezing my breath out. It grew less or more, but it was there, it went on and on. Karl and Mara, Mara and Karl. I couldn't get those hands of his out of my mind. I woke up that night, hot and cold all over, having had a dream where Karl and Mara and I were hiding and hunting, but who was hunting whom I didn't know. It was all mixed up. And there in the dark bed at night, as always happens, all the past began to come back, hateful, acrid like something vomited, and I tried to sleep again and could not.

Two days later we had a quarrel, violent, but made up quickly. I don't remember how it began, but then I passed a remark about how nice it was to be provided for. She didn't answer, she looked at me and then away. I then said lots of things, horrible things which I can't remember. She just kept looking away.

I stopped. 'Well, I must get back. Can't dawdle today I'm afraid, got something else to do,' and tried to leave her, she so silent; to run away from her, but that was not possible. So I stood, immobile, in the cold street, wanting to go away, wanting to remain. And then I said, 'Oh, Mara, I'm a bloody idiot.'

And she said: 'Oh, Red, why d'you always want to hit out at things and people?'

I said: 'I don't know.'

And so we made it up.

Then Andy began making passes again. He was swotting for his finals, and that kept him more in his room at Nancy's. At about midnight he'd scratch on my door. I locked myself in every night. And the next morning he would make remarks about spinsters.

One day Mara said: 'Karl's gone to the Continent for a week, come to my place.'

That evening I went back to her flat with her, and we had coffee and toast and eggs, and laughed and were happy, wonderfully happy.

'Have you done more painting?' I asked.

She said yes, but didn't offer to show me. And I didn't ask to see. 'I'll paint you, one day, Red,' she said.

'Thanks,' I said, 'that'll be a laugh.'

She sat opposite me and started sketching, but when I wanted to look she didn't show me. 'Some other time,' she said.

But I never saw it.

While Karl was away Mara began to speak about him to me. And it was obvious she did not like him. 'He's really a kind of black marketeer, except that he's a respectable one. Travels in liberated Europe, making business connections.' She smiled briefly. 'The democratic reconstruction of Europe. France is full of businessmen, American mostly, dressed up as colonels and generals, with ladders of medals climbing up and down their chests. And people like Karl do business with them. They call it putting things back on their feet. It keeps Karl very busy.'

During the days Karl was away I went every evening to Mara's flat, and stayed later and later. There was a nice kitchen, and things to eat like Jerusalem artichokes and tinned peaches and tins from Fortnum's which cost the earth, and new-laid eggs from a friend of Karl's in the country.

'Lovely grub,' I said to Mara.

Mara laughed and laughed. It always made her laugh when I talked like that, as lots of us did at the Horsham now, in keeping with the times. Mara didn't talk like that, she didn't even listen to *Itma* on the radio, but she laughed when I did it and that made me feel good.

Mara was quite extravagant; when a tin was half used she'd throw the rest away. Once I rescued some anchovies which she'd discarded.

'You're so thrifty, Red,' Mara laughed. 'I just don't like left-overs.'

'We're at war,' I said pointedly.

And Mara said: 'Oh, yes,' guiltily, and after that she was more careful.

But the word thrifty hurt because I'd been called something like that before, by my stepmother; yet, God knows, with Mara I wasn't, I didn't want to be.

But apart from expensive things, there wasn't much solid food around. 'We eat out a lot, Karl and I,' she said.

Mara did not bother to cook much, but when she did it was like a banquet. One day we bought a goose, as geese came on sale just before Christmas. It cost the earth, and Mara roasted it in the oven, and we ate as much of it as we could; but there was far too much, and after two days she gave the rest to the char.

I was horrified. 'A family could have eaten for a week.'

'Her family will,' she replied.

Walking back from Mara's flat to Nancy's boarding-house was going from one world to another, but I wasn't jealous of Mara's comfort, I was pleased and proud to have a friend so well-off. Not that I myself wouldn't be well-off one day: my father had left some money in trust for me, I'd get it when I was twenty-one. Meanwhile I had an allowance. Then there was Aunt Muriel. Aunt Muriel always said that everything she had would come to me. And I had a great-aunt up north; she was a bit queer, and might leave her all to a cats' and dogs' home, so I didn't bank too much on it. Meanwhile, I rather pigged it. I had to be careful with money, one never knew what might happen, and I saved about a third of my allowance because I might need it. The way Mara took taxis, bought books, went to expensive places ... whatever she had was expensive. I thought with pleasure, though, that I had a rich friend. I did not know that she could walk out of money and comfort as easily as losing a handkerchief (and she was always losing handkerchiefs). She dazzled me a little, I had not been accustomed to this kind of spending.

From Mara's flat to Nancy's boarding-house I went back at night by bus and then trolley-bus up to Camden Town, a long, long way. Mara sometimes came with me. The statue of Cobden loomed in the darkness as if to bar the way. I'd never taken Mara beyond it. When we got there, we'd catch a bus and go all the way back to Mayfair.

'It's still a long way,' I told her one day when she said: 'How far from Cobden do you live, Red?' 'It's much farther, and there's no dinner for you at the end I'm afraid. You'll have to go home for it, and that'll mean my trotting back with you.' I said it half joking, half earnest, I didn't want her to see where I lived.

From Cobden there was another four hundred yards, a long, dismal row of houses, one of which was Nancy's. The houses were all alike, angular, spinsterish, narrow, an architecture whose dreary repetition became hallucinatory. Even on the brightest day they wore mute discouragement in every lineament of their façade. The windows were not conceived to admit light or air, so blindly forbidding their outward bleakness. All the houses must have smelt the same as Nancy's did, from the narrow hall-way with the grime-worn lino, down the steps into the basement dining room, up the stairs to the rooms on the first and second floors and the attic, all smelt of stale cigarettes, cat, dirt, cabbage and dustbins.

At Nancy's lived Edward, of course, the travelling salesman, who had been a keen Y.M.C.A. gym teacher. But he was blind as a bat, and the Forces didn't want him. He smelt of sweat even after a bath, and the bathroom smelt of sweat too because he used to do Swedish exercises in it, and then use the toilet. His conversation never left the topic of his muscles and his regular habits, no laxatives needed. Because of Edward I'd given up using the main bathroom in the morning, and took turns at the small W.C. at the top of the house. There was Andy, the son of a colonial bishop, doing medicine on a colonial medical scholarship because his father was a prelate in Singapore. He was not always present at our lino-covered festive board. His absences were the subject of elaborate and not at all obscure joking on the part of Edward and Nancy, the general idea being that Andy was a 'gay dog'; it was understood that he had been passionately loved by a White Russian, and was now pursued by a Free French woman, who would throw herself under the next trolley-bus for his sake. I didn't believe in her existence, and still don't, knowing Andy. Edward was Nancy's occasional lover, when she felt well enough between her fits of gastric acidity, deploring the war, and being upset over Winston the cat, who had been named thus under false pretences, and remained Winston after six litters because Nancy felt it unpatriotic to change. All of us boarders hated Winston, but we couldn't do anything about her, until one day Nancy fell suddenly with a loud cry on the floor after lifting the milk jug away from Winston's whisking tail. She had perforated her gastric ulcer. She was removed to St Thomas's because Andy took charge, was operated on, and was back in six weeks. During those six weeks we did for ourselves, in turn taking over the kitchen. That was when Andy had got at me, and I let him, we'd been doing the washing-up together, and then gone to the pub for some beer, and it seemed unsporting not to.

When Nancy came back, Winston came back too. We'd banished her during meals, but with Nancy's return she stalked among our plates, and once more cat-hair floated like scum on the morning milk jug.

That was where I lived. I was used to it, but I didn't want Mara to see it. Until now I'd liked my digs because they were dirt-cheap, but now that I saw how Mara lived I began to think of something better. A place where I could ask Mara. I could afford it.

Now I felt I must prove to Mara I wasn't too thrifty, as she had said. It made me feel bad too because of my great-aunt in the north, who was reputed to be a real miser, and I didn't want to become like her. And my step had always been at me, about hoarding things, because at one time I'd kept all the bits of string I could find, and tied them together in one long string.

I walked in Camden Town, back to my digs, and every time the smell in the corridor came to hit me in the face, I thought: I must find some other place. Where I can ask Mara to come.

* * *

One afternoon in mid-December it was milder, lighter. At four o'clock we walked away from the Horsham, dawdling as if it were spring.

'Let's have tea at Maggie's,' I suggested.

Maggie's was a small place off James Street. Before the war there had been wonderful buns and cakes, but now we only got some 'yellow perils', buns made with egg powder, with imitation caraway-seeds on top. I liked Maggie's because it was cosy, in spite of war. Maggie herself looked after the shop. She was a big woman, with a high, tired voice and large varicose knots in her legs. It was Louise who had taken me to Maggie's first, but now I took Mara and Louise didn't come with me any more.

We were early. There was no one yet at Maggie's, the office-workers hadn't come out of their offices. It was warm inside the small tea-shop, basking in almost green light, a liquid submarine glow from the bow window with its bottle-glass panes. It was wonderful to stretch one's legs, sitting beside Mara, as good as being in her flat with her: one felt submerged, enveloped, floating, tranquil as seaweed and as compliant. Here, in a sea-water absolution, with the stirring smell of hot buns, it might even be better than in Mara's flat, because here was no Karl entering, bringing unease with him, and a fear something might suddenly go bang, like a concealed gun with an unsure trigger.

' 'Afternoon, Maggie.'

'Nice day,' said Maggie, 'turned warm all of a sudden, like. Cold again tomorrow though, I shouldn't wonder.' Maggie dropped the subject and went back to get us tea. She had the gift of leaving people alone and comfortable with themselves. Her remarks about the weather she suspended in mid-air, take it or leave it. One didn't have to strike poses.

The radio was on, not too loud. There was a drone afar off, a buzz-bomb; I'd been doing some fire-watching the week before, and one had gone overhead and stopped quite a way off.

'There she blows,' said Maggie, putting down the tea-pot and two cups, and going back for buns. 'A doodle-bug last night near where I live. We spent half the night digging one bloke out, got himself cooped up in the basement. No other damage, I'm glad to say.'

This one was coming near. We lifted our heads. Very near now, it seemed just above us, and the vibration made the crockery rattle on the counter. Then the motor cut out.

'Mind your 'eads,' cried Maggie, diving under the counter.

Mara and I were both under our table when it fell, a whoosh so deafening it wasn't noise but a shaking and splintering and sucking of all the air round, then the instantaneous dust swirling eddies thick as cloth, making us cough and know we were alive.

Though the memory of that moment of terror is precise enough, I don't remember any particular, overwhelming fear at the instant when the buzz-bomb fell; only a stunned, nearly surprised joy and relief that I was still alive afterwards. Then Mara's face, thick with dust, featureless like one of those weather-worn statues in an old square. In the bronze blob the eyes began to move, ludicrously. I wanted to laugh with relief. We were both alive.

'Are you all right?' I said.

'Yes, I'm all right. Are you?'

'Yes.'

And then suddenly there were a lot of people, bringing with them a panic of emotions, terror, horror. We were picked up bodily, my legs now swaying under me and my heart racing, but there was also an enormous triumphant feeling in me as if I had just done something wonderful. People kept crowding round and asking if we were all right, and Mara and I were struggling not to be conveyed to stretchers, shaking our heads, slapping the dust away from our clothes, wiping our faces on towels that appeared. There was an ambulance, uniformed ambulance attendants, someone came up to me and asked if I wanted a shock injection, I said crossly: 'For God's sake, I'm all right I tell you.'

And now, the counter off, there also was Maggie. I think Mara saw her before I did, because she said: 'Oh –' very short, put a hand to her mouth. But it took me time after looking to see what was the matter, a lag between what I saw and heard and

37

knowing what it was. There was some dark liquid on the floor, like coffee-grounds, which at first didn't make sense, then Maggie's sprawled legs with their disfiguring blue veins intact, and in her neck a jutting piece of green glass. The ambulance people had the blanket quick over her, head and all.

But death was only a word which I said to myself, a word without savour. Mara was clinging to me and saying: 'Red, let's go,' shaking my arm. She took my arm and turned me from looking at Maggie's stretcher, now heaved into the ambulance.

Though it must have been only minutes it seemed hours, giving our names, telling a lot of people we were quite all right, before we were out in the dark streets. And now there was another ambulance, and stretchers going up and down full or empty, and I remember saying, 'Can I help?' because that was the right thing to do, and Mara whispering fiercely: 'NO, no, let's go. For God's sake, let's get away.'

And the A.R.P. man saying: 'Well, ducks, you've had quite enough, off with you,' and a man coming up again to say: 'Sure you don't need a shock injection?' and Mara saying again: 'Let's go home.'

I could see that the A.R.P. man thought Mara was a foreigner. He was immediately soothing, saying to me: 'You'd better take her home, she's had quite a shock.'

And Mara whispered: 'Let's go home, let's go home,' not a bit brave or anything.

I felt conspicuous because of Mara not being brave and not offering to help, so I said, 'O.K., pull yourself together, we're going.'

But the A.R.P. man said sharply: 'Now, don't fuss her, miss. Your friend's upset, can't you see?' And that was unfair to me, I thought.

Mara was silent till we got to the corner of her street. Then she tugged my hand, pulling me back, and said: 'I don't want to go there.' She began to walk away, and I had to follow her.

I said to her: 'You've been shouting "I want to go home," I see you home, then you don't want to go home. What *do* you want?'

She said: 'We'll go to your place. Where you live. Let's go there.'

Then I became angry, and frightened. I didn't want her to come to my place. What on earth for? I could have had such a nice bath in her place, and heaven knows I needed it. But at the same time, dimly, there was a kind of excitement in me as if I were shaking inside of myself; at the pit of my stomach tumult and clamour. I could hear my own voice being angry, but even as I spoke the anger went away into this uneasy excitement. I was now following Mara down the street, arguing with her. 'Look, Mara, what's come over you? Honest, Mara, it's so silly. My place isn't half as good as yours. You – we both need a clean-up. I'd like a good bath, my pet. Mara … '

She walked fast, I had to continue following her. A taxi was coming down the street, Mara stepped down in the road in front of it, waving her hand. The driver stopped, brakes crunching, leaned out and began to shout his annoyance. But she smiled at him, and he smiled back, mollified. She opened the door.

'Get in, Red,' she said. She gave the man my address.

'Now look here,' I began, 'now look here, you'll have to pay – '

But the taxi man was looking at me, and I am scared of scenes in public. Off we drove. I thought: it's no use Mara trying to bully me like that. When we get to the door I'll say good night. She'll have to go back alone, all the way to Mayfair. I'm damned if I'll see her home tonight.

As we turned sharply into Oxford Street the traffic hurtled its noise at us like the blast of the buzz-bomb, and all my anger swept out of me. I wanted to put my head down and weep. Maggie was dead, and here we were, driving in a taxi, and I could feel the dust in my hair, round my neck, between my fingers. But still it mattered that Mara shouldn't see my room, I was a fool not to have moved into a nice place before, even if I had to pay more. I *would* turn round and say goodbye at the door.

When we reached the door of Nancy's boarding-house Mara paid the taxi, and I pleaded: 'Mara, it's an awful place.' (The smell, the cat, Nancy, Andy. Mara would *never* want to see me again once she knew how I lived.)

'Let's go to your room and sit down.'

'O.K., if you insist. But you won't like it.'

Nancy was out (her coat wasn't hanging in the hall), which was a bit of luck. Nancy is rather a busybody, poking her face out of the basement dining room door and watching who is going up or down stairs.

'Upstairs, second floor,' I said.

We went up, treading lightly, her steps exactly in front of mine, mine timed to hers so that if anyone listened they would not hear two people going up at the same time. On the sixth step I used to kick the seventh for luck. Not this time. I opened the door of my room, turning the knob gently, slowly, feeling it turn. I pressed the light switch. The less noise, the better. Well, that was the worst that could happen.

'I like your room.'

The worst was over, and I couldn't help anything from now on.

She went to the deep armchair (the springs sagged, the cover was dirt-brown), and sat down.

'I'll put on the gas-fire.'

I felt her watching me as I took the match box, knelt to put a shilling in the gas-meter, a match to the hissing holes; with a pop the blue flames licked up. To face her I sat on the edge of the bed. Her coat was dusty, her face none too clean. 'We both look like wrecks,' I said.

'We are,' she replied.

Downstairs the gong sounded for supper. 'Call to the festive board,' I said.

'You go,' Mara said. 'I'll wait here.'

'I can't go looking like this,' I said, 'and I'm not hungry anyway.'

I didn't like going down, with Andy, Edward, and possibly Nancy back at the head of the table presiding over the soup. I leaned back on the bed. My hand fingered the blue tweed blanket which I kept on top. I told Mara: 'My Daddy gave me this blanket.'

'Did he, Red?'

'Yes.' I became a child, lapsing into near baby-talk. Mara was my mother, and I was drowsy, and telling her things I wanted to tell. 'I loved my Daddy. He was nice to me. Even when my step told him the most horrid things about me—that I should be psychoanalysed, that I was queer, that I collected bits of string and that showed I wasn't normal – even then he was nice to me. "Never mind," he would say, "you'll be all right. Daddy knows it. That's my girl," he used to say. I hate my step and she loathes me. I hope she dies of cancer, or something terrible happens to her. But my Daddy loved me, I know it.'

'I love you too, Red,' said Mara gently.

I did not answer.

'It is difficult, Red,' said Mara. 'I am a woman and you are a woman. I am a grown-up woman, with a husband, and I've always been what is called normal. I've never felt like this about … about any other woman.'

I could hear Edward's booming laugh, and a clatter of crockery.

'When I say I love you, I mean, not like a friend.' Mara was speaking as if far from herself, level-voiced. 'This between us, can you call it friendship? I mean, do you think the other couples of women we see around us are only friends?'

'Yes, of course,' I burst out, 'definitely. You're wrong there, you're making up things in your mind. They're just crushes. It isn't what you mean. It isn't.'

'Perhaps you are right. Perhaps it is as you say. This is a funny time,' she mused. 'I get such a woman feeling, such a feminine, woman-world-only feeling here. Perhaps it's the war. It must be. Perhaps it's imagination. I don't know. But men seem effaced somehow ... they don't really exist, except when I walk in Piccadilly, where it's just rank with them. But I don't think I like men.'

'Don't imagine things, Mara. At the Horsham most of the girls you see going about in twos will get married, and they'll be quite all right. Even Louise.'

'Why even Louise?'

'Oh, I was at school with Louise,' I said. 'But she's quite all right, really. She'll hook a man and she'll be fine.'

I couldn't tell Mara about Louise. How Louise was one of my girls, in a way. She'd wanted it: made me hit her and kiss her and handle her breasts, while she uttered little cries and her big eyes rolled. But it wasn't really very serious. Mara was too clean for that, I felt. I didn't want her to know.

'Look,' I said, and tried to keep my voice from shaking, 'maybe some of us do do a bit of substitution. But it's mostly emotional. It's natural for a girl to have crushes on other girls, hold hands and all that.' I got angry. 'You've got the Continental viewpoint. Comes from marrying a Swiss. You look at everything from a sex point of view. It's not, I tell you. There isn't that much libido around.'

'I wouldn't know,' said Mara, 'where pure emotion, a crush as you say, stops and sex begins. Does anyone know? When does a feeling become a sin? When the body performs what is already formed in the mind? Tell me that, Red?'

'Quite the philosopher, aren't you?' I parried. So many things could be done, and if one didn't talk about them, didn't think about them, one could live with them, they would be quite all right. But when put in words they came barging into one's consciousness at all times, and one knew the foulness of deeds. But not before they'd been put in words. So the important thing was not to call things by their names. 'I wouldn't know,' I said, 'I'm not a psychologist, Mara.'

She said: 'I want to know why I have this feeling about you. I'm concerned to know what it is makes me want to be with you so much. I've never felt like this before, and I don't understand myself.'

'I don't know what you mean,' I lied, my voice trembling.

'You do know, Red. And I want to know.'

'Look,' I said, 'maybe I've had a hard time, see. Maybe you haven't. You've always got everything you wanted, I suppose. You're older than I am, you've got experience, and you're rich. I don't want to start anything. I want to be normal. I am normal. I want to have men, I want to get married.'

She sat in profound attention, pondering, and with her next words things came into focus again: like looking down a microscope at a blur, then you turn a gadget and the proper focus comes on and everything is sharp and clear.

'Red,' she said, 'I don't want to *start* anything. That's why I'm asking you, why do I feel like this? I've never felt like this about a *woman* before.'

43

I lay back on the bed. Life was one great big treachery. Here I was back where I had not meant to be. Face to face with something I hadn't wanted to know. I looked up, and for the first time I noticed the ceiling of my room and the electric-light bulb with its round white shade suspended from the cord in the middle. Like an umbilical cord. I played for a moment with the idea that the lamp hanging like that in the middle of nothing from a string was a baby, and the baby was me. A small sprouting of life in the middle of nothing, tied to the womb of the past, tied by all the things that had been done and not said. And if you cut that cord, the lamp fell, the light went out.

And Mara said: 'This has happened to you before, Red, but not to me.'

How did she know? I'd never said anything.

'It was the games mistress, Mara. She'd been jilted by her young man. She took it out on me.' I raised myself on my elbow, acting flippant. 'It's always the games mistress or the English Lit. mistress, didn't you know? Or some senior girl. It's done in the best schools, m'dear.'

'Did you feel bad about it?'

'Not really.' Suddenly I saw her very clearly, Rhoda, my games mistress, fair curly hair cut short at the nape, pretty face, petulant mouth, blue frock with bosom-fitting lace. Now it seemed childish, ridiculous, yet dirty. That pouting mouth was stupid, that trick of hers of winking one eye at me which I had liked so much was stupid. Louise's eyes too were stupid. And I had called them blue interlopers when I was reading Shelley.

'Red, don't cry, please don't cry,' said Mara.

I was crying, I realized with astonishment. Tears ran down my face, my palm upon my face came off moist and shining like sweat under the lamplight.

She came over to the bed. 'Lie down,' she said, 'lie down. Lie down, my darling.'

'She said that she would be my mother. A mother to me. That's what she said.'

'She lied,' said Mara, 'but I'm not going to lie to you. I am not going to be your mother, Red. I just love you, that is all, and why I should love you I don't know.'

And somehow it was simple and right and beautiful and good this time when she put her arms round me and we were kissing, and could not stop though there was dust between our lips.

*   *   *

Christmas holidays meant Aunt Muriel. Aunt Muriel was my father's younger sister, and my nearest relative. I had spent Christmas holidays with Aunt Muriel for the past four years, nobody else seemed to want me, and in wartime there was no other place I could go to.

Aunt Muriel lived in Wiltshire, on a farm near the village of Abbots, seven miles outside Salisbury. She was on the station platform in her W.V.S. uniform, slapping her thigh with her riding-crop, when our train drew in. Almost as long as I can remember Aunt Muriel had a stick in her hand, using it to point at things on her farm, or to slap herself with; I think it gave her a sense of authority, of power. When I scrambled out of the train she looked at my shoes. She has a passion for highly-polished shoes, she thought mine weren't so good.

'Hallo, Aunt Muriel. My, how you've grown.'

She smiled. Aunt Muriel likes to be teased as if she were still a little girl in pigtails. 'Go on with you,' she said. 'Have you got your luggage down, dear? Good. Right, we'll go along then,

I've got the station-wagon. It'll be a tight squeeze but you won't mind, will you?'

There were ten pairs of Wellington boots, a sack of chicken-feed, a saddle, two buckets, and on the front seat at the wheel, Rhoda. The last person I wanted to see. Of course, Aunt Muriel would ask Rhoda. She'd been there last Christmas, and the Christmas before that. That was my doing. I'd arranged it myself three years ago, and it had now become a fixture. Aunt Muriel thought a lot of Rhoda. She'd never known about Rhoda and me. She thought we were good friends, she'd thought that for years, ever since Rhoda, who's about ten years older than I am, was my games mistress at school. Aunt Muriel had come down to the school one Visitors' Day and Rhoda had rushed up to her and started telling her what an excellent sport, unspoilt and *healthy-minded* girl I was. That was music to Aunt Muriel's ears because she hated my step and my step had been telling her that I was abnormal and ought to be psycho-analysed. But now it was my step who was abnormal, taking up first Christian Science and then going on to spirit-mediumship, and now she kept on sending Aunt Muriel pamphlets about the dear departed. Aunt Muriel couldn't stand the idea of death, so anything that was against my step became all right with her. Aunt Muriel took to Rhoda, and after that Rhoda was asked to stay for Christmas. 'Rhoda's such a good influence on Bettina,' said Aunt Muriel to her friends.

'Well,' said Aunt Muriel jovially, 'shove in, Bettina. You sit between Rhoda and me, as you did last year, remember?'

'Bettina,' said Rhoda, with that healthy, fresh and sparkling voice she used, which I'd thought wonderful and now was like a dose of Eno's fruit salts, 'so *good* to see you, m'dear.'

'Hallo, Rhoda,' I said. I sat down, hating the way she sat. I had to shove my arm in so that my coat sleeve touched hers, and

46

even that was embarrassing. We had always been careful, casual in our greetings, taking pains not to notice each other, so people wouldn't get suspicious as they did about others I knew of. So it wasn't too difficult to turn away from Rhoda, talk to Aunt Muriel, find questions to ask about the farm, and the Poles and the evacuees in Abbots, since Aunt Muriel was head of the committee for the latter. Rhoda started the car. She drove, Aunt Muriel chattered on, I pretended to be terribly interested in all she said although I didn't hear half of it: Aunt Muriel can go on for hours about what interests her, so conversation is easy with her. All the time I thought: I hope Aunt Muriel doesn't put us in the same room, as last year.

But Aunt Muriel had put us in the same room, as she pointed out when we got to the house. 'You know the way, Bettina.'

I left my suitcase in the passage, and while Rhoda parked the car I tackled Aunt Muriel, who was already in the kitchen. 'Aunt Muriel?'

'Yes. What is it, Bettina?'

'I … it's … Aunt Muriel, I don't sleep very well, and I've got to swot. Exams next year, you know. I thought perhaps … d'you mind if I go in the spare room this year?'

'That's quite impossible, Bettina,' said Aunt Muriel. 'I thought I told you in the station-wagon about my new Polish help and her infant. They're in the spare bedroom. She's a D.P., a wonderful cook. I couldn't put her in the maid's room, it's much too small for the infant, and she'd leave me flat – you know how it is these days.'

'Well, can I have the maid's room, then?'

Aunt Muriel wasn't pleased. 'I'm afraid you can't. It's full of W.V.S. stores. I'm sure Rhoda won't make a fuss, even if you do study. And I'll give you one of my sleeping-pills.'

So there was nothing to be done, and I had to drag my suitcase into the room Rhoda and I would share, and start unpacking; and while I was at it Rhoda came in, smoking a cigarette. The room smelt of her. I pretended to be busy putting my things in a drawer.

Rhoda came and stood behind me. 'Bettybets,' she said, and put a hand on my shoulder, 'what's the matter? Having the grumpies?'

'There's nothing the matter,' I said, busily sorting my things into the drawer.

She kept her hand on my shoulder, and I couldn't go on keeping mine inside the drawer, so I closed the drawer slowly and turned round to my suitcase, and her hand dropped.

She walked to the bed and lay back on it, pulling on her cigarette and watching me. 'You didn't write much, last few weeks,' she said. 'I was expecting a letter from you.'

'I've been very busy,' I said.

'Red,' said Rhoda, 'don't act that way, darling. Please come and tell your Rho-Rho you're glad to see her.'

'Of course I am,' I said. 'But you know I'm going to be pretty busy now, I've got a lot of swotting to do.'

'Has anybody said anything?' said Rhoda, sitting up straight. 'Because it isn't true, Red. I mean, nobody else means anything to me.'

So there had been someone around. For a moment I thought it would be a good thing to act jealous. I'd been really jealous once about Rhoda. I shrugged my shoulders. 'Skip it,' I said. 'Of course one hears things.'

'Angela doesn't mean a thing to me,' said Rhoda. 'Not a thing, Red, you must believe me.'

'Well,' I said, still keeping that weary and worn look on my face, 'let's skip it, shall we? We've all got to grow up.'

I was breathing more easily now. I could even look at Rhoda

sitting on the edge of the bed. There was a night-table between her bed and what would be mine.

'Red, you know no one else means ... what you mean to me.'

She was plainly worried now. I could remember everything between Rhoda and me. I was sixteen, she was twenty-six, and something had just happened to her – she'd been jilted by her fiancé. I was big for my age, and lonely. She said she wanted to be a mother to me. Rhoda had used me, and taught me, and now I was what I was because of her. I wanted to shout at her, to hit her as she sat there looking at me out of her big blue eyes, afraid. She had on a blue dress, wool. I remembered the letters I'd written to her, and those she'd written to me, and that horrible June when I loved her and she loved someone else.

'You know jolly well,' she said, 'that I love you, Red. You and I, it's *different*, darling.'

I laughed, I couldn't help it. I remembered that summer when she no longer whispered: 'See you tonight.' No more little notes: 'The coast is clear.' Twice I'd gone to her room, knocking softly, lonely, sick at heart. The first time she made some tea, light conversation; then yawned: 'Well, nighty-night, darling, I'm so tired ... such a hot, tiring day ... see you soon.' A peck. No longer those deep, searching kisses that she had first taught me, that used to leave me shaken and spent. The second time she was annoyed: 'Darling, I'm sorry, I was sleeping. Come in if you wish, but we must be careful, you know.'

And on the following Sunday I saw her with a man, a red-faced, bull-necked fellow, walking in the woods near school. I'd been to the woods on my bicycle to pick flowers for her. She was wearing blue frock with the lace frills round the bosom.

And now she wore blue, quite a nice dress, and I couldn't bring myself to think of touching her. Though I'd sobbed with happiness when she'd taken me back a couple of years ago.

49

She'd sworn there was nothing, nothing between the man and her. Then she'd been quite sick for a while.

There'd been Louise, in an off-and-on way, but not really much: Louise was too bitchy, she just liked being hurt a bit. But there was Mara. And Mara was everything. I was in love, truly in love.

'Don't laugh, Red,' pleaded Rhoda, 'I do mean it.'

'Oh, for heaven's sake,' I said, 'don't be melodramatic.'

'You've *changed*, Red,' Rhoda said, like a bad line in a bad play.

'Of course I've changed,' I replied. 'I've grown up, I keep telling you.'

She crushed her cigarette then, she was going to cry, and I went on putting my things in the drawers.

'I see,' she said, and her voice was tired. 'You've grown. It's not me that's changed, it's you. Who's the lucky man? Do I know him?'

'No,' I said, enormously relieved that Rhoda had made it simple, 'I'm afraid you don't. I tell you, Rhoda, I've grown up.'

On the next day the local school had a carol service. Aunt Muriel, Rhoda and I went to it, and I nearly fell asleep in the church. I hadn't slept much that night, Rhoda in the next bed, both of us not talking. I'd undressed in the bathroom, and all kinds of things kept cropping up in my memory, intensely disagreeable. Getting up, Rhoda had made morning tea (she always did for Aunt Muriel, and that was another reason why Aunt Muriel liked her so much: Rhoda really pulled her weight doing chores as a guest during the holidays).

'I've made tea for you, Red,' said Rhoda.

And I had to say: 'Thanks,' and jump out of bed quickly and get to the bathroom to stop any attempted conversation.

At church it was better. I thought of Mara and hoped there would be a letter the next day. I'd asked her to write to me.

Before church we had done the chicken-feed, Rhoda and I, as we'd done in previous holidays. There were lamb chops for lunch, and chocolate fudge as a special treat, and Rhoda and I washed up. We didn't talk much to each other, but Aunt Muriel didn't notice, she was so glad she had helping hands to do the housework, especially over Christmas.

Rhoda was very good about things that morning, and apart from making conversation with Aunt Muriel of the do-you-remember kind and about how badly the Poles in the camp behaved, she didn't try anything woozily sentimental, so that by the time lunch was over the atmosphere was better. As long as one didn't linger on what had been and remember things, one could sound chummy and cosy, and that's how it was meant to be.

The telephone rang. Rhoda got up and said: 'I'll go, Aunt Muriel.' Taking care of phone-calls was Rhoda's job, and driving the station-wagon because Aunt Muriel said Rhoda was so economical with the petrol. Actually Aunt Muriel was a bit frightened of telephones and cars.

Rhoda came back from the passage where the telephone was. 'It's for you,' she said to me. She sat down without looking at me.

I got up, pretending to be surprised, with a who-on-earth-could-that-be look on my face. But I felt panicky and I knew I was blushing, so I turned my face quickly away, at the same time telling myself not to hurry too much or they might suspect; and though I wanted to run down the passage to the telephone because I was afraid the call might be disconnected, I forced myself to walk, my heart pounding because I knew, I was sure it was Mara.

It was Mara, all the way from London, of course it was. She alone would do a mad and wonderful thing like that, ringing me up. No one else ever did things like that for me. I always had had to do the ringing up and the asking, and going to people's rooms, always I was the one to ask for love.

'Bettina Jones?' said the operator. 'Call from London.'

'Hallo?' said Mara's voice. 'Is that you, Red?'

'Yes,' I replied, 'yes. Is that you, Mara?'

'Yes,' said Mara, 'it's me.'

I could see her hanging on to the telephone in London, just as I was here at Aunt Muriel's in Wiltshire, and it was absurd, we had nothing to say except: 'How are you?' and: 'Very well, and you?' I answered: 'Very well,' and she said: 'That's fine,' and I said: 'Are you all right?' I could have kicked myself for wasting the precious and irreplaceable time being inane.

She said: 'Did you have a good journey?'

And I said: 'Yes, it's nice out here. Lots of grub.'

Then there was another long pause, and I thought I could hear her breathe, then the instrument went pip pip pip, and the operator said: 'Have you finished, or do you want to extend the call?'

I heard Mara say: 'Extend.'

We hung on, and I said: 'How's London?' and she said: 'All right,' and I said: 'That's fine.'

And so another three minutes went by, and we spoke about the weather in London and in Salisbury, and again the instrument went pip pip pip, and again Mara's voice said: 'Extend,' and I said: 'This is getting terribly expensive, isn't it?' and she said: 'Red, do you read Blake?'

The telephone started to crackle.

'Read Blake?' I repeated. 'Why?'

'D'you know that thing of Blake's,' she said, "Tiger, tiger, burning bright in the forests of the night"? That was a real live tiger, Red,' she said, 'lovely and striped with black and yellow, Red, a real tropical tiger.'

'What's that got to do with it?' I asked.

'With what?' she said.

'Oh, with everything,' I said. 'I don't understand.'

'It doesn't,' she said. 'That's why. It's just a way of saying how are you, talking of tigers. Perhaps one day we'll go to the jungles and see real tigers.'

'Listen,' I said, 'is this supposed to be funny? It isn't funny to pour money down the drain ringing me up long-distance to talk about tigers.'

'You mean, down the telephone,' she said. 'Don't you like tigers?'

'No,' I said, and suddenly I was angry and hurt. This wasn't at all what I had expected, but then what did I expect? Talking about tigers, and there I was, stuck with Rhoda stalking me. 'No,' I nearly shouted, 'I don't like tigers.'

Three pips.

'Time's up,' said the operator.

'Well, goodbye Red,' said Mara. 'See you soon.' And she hung up.

I swore under my breath, and I stayed there staring at the heartless black telephone on its hook. And now I wanted to say: come back, oh come back, only let me hear your voice again, your voice talking about tigers, beautiful tigers. But it was too late to tell Mara that I understood about tigers, or even elephants, that I would love a giraffe if she spoke about giraffes. And why had I become so angry suddenly? Perhaps because with Mara, or because of Mara, I was always being made to remember things that I thought I'd forgotten, or wanted to forget ... like my mother. And now I knew. That afternoon in the Zoo, when I was five, or maybe six, my mother and a man talking to each other, in front of the tigers' cage, and I, beribboned, with mittens, I wanted to pee, and I was scared of the terrible smell of the tigers; and there was my mother laughing, her face rosy under a big hat, with that man whose face I would never remember because I hated him so much, his hand tugging at her gloved hand.

When I came back Rhoda was sitting with her back quite rigid, and Aunt Muriel said comfortably: 'Who was it, dear?'

I said: 'Just a friend, wanting some of my Organic notes.' That was enough for Aunt Muriel, and as for Rhoda I didn't care. She won't try anything, I told myself. I took Blake's *Complete Works* down from the book-shelves where Aunt Muriel had it along with other Complete Works.

I went round all afternoon in anguished happiness, then as it grew dark I became unhappy and restless, repeating tiger, tiger. So many days before I could see Mara again. Why, yielding to habit, had I come to Aunt Muriel's instead of staying a few more days in London? It was only the twentieth, five days to Christmas. Couldn't I have come, say, on the twenty-third? That would have been three days, three days more with Mara. I could have done it, it wouldn't have hurt anybody, I could have told Aunt Muriel that I was busy swotting. She wouldn't have minded too much. I hadn't thought of it that way before leaving London. Aunt Muriel was my relative, she'd be leaving me all her money, I should be nice to the old girl, give her a bit of my young time and company in the holidays, which meant doing the chickens and washing the dishes and helping clean the house, and doing the fires on alternate days. So I'd come on the twentieth as usual, sheer force of habit. Sometimes I had to remember that Aunt Muriel also *liked* me, and didn't only ask me to help out on the farm. It wasn't fair to think of it that way. There was a war on. Before supper I went down to the kitchen to help the Polish girl peel potatoes and do the sprouts, and later I shut up the chickens. And all the time I longed for Mara so much I felt quite ill.

After dinner, with the blackout curtains carefully drawn, we sat round the fire. Rhoda did *The Times* crossword puzzle while Aunt Muriel did the W.V.S. accounts. I wanted to go up to the bedroom and write to Mara, but it was jolly cold upstairs, the other two might suspect, or Rhoda might say something catty about me to Aunt. By leaving the room I would break up the picture of cosiness, of us three women peaceful round the hearth, each doing her bit for the country. So I sat on, pretending to read my physiology notes (I made a show of having to swot). By pretending to read, keeping a book open in my hands, I needn't talk, I could dream to my heart's content. And so I sat, lost in a dream of Mara, and I didn't know what was happening around me until I heard Aunt Muriel's voice saying: 'What are you smiling at, Bettina? Is it a novel?' Aunt Muriel thinks all novels should contain some passage funny enough to smile at, though naturally never coarse.

I was brought back to the present, to Rhoda watching me with narrowed eyes. I felt Rhoda knew I had lied to her, that she was wondering about the phone-call. Perhaps if you've loved someone and they've loved you, some telepathic understanding remains, so that she was aware I hadn't told the truth, just as I was aware that she knew it. Anyway, I found myself going red, and I said: 'I was half alseep. Think I'll toddle off to bed now. 'Night, Aunt Muriel. 'Night, Rhoda.'

If Rhoda didn't come up too soon, but stayed downstairs with Aunt Muriel, I would have some time alone, some time to dream of Mara.

* * *

The next morning Mara's telegram was phoned through by the Post Office, but I didn't know it as I was with the chickens.

It was Rhoda who took the message over the telephone, and I didn't get it until an hour later. Of course she did that purposely. It happened that she was in the house and heard the phone ring when I'd already gone down to the chicken-run. Instead of coming to tell me about the message, she disappeared; one hour later, when I went upstairs to wash my hands, I found the piece of paper in the bedroom with Mara's message: 'Arriving eleven-twenty train tomorrow Mara.'

I was furious. That was a rotten thing to do to me, and of course Rhoda had done it purposely, and now she knew I'd lied to her and that it wasn't a man. I leapt to the telephone and rang up the Post Office. They told me that the telegram had been sent the night before from London, so 'tomorrow' on the message meant today, meant now. Of course it was just like Mara to write a vague tomorrow instead of putting the date.

She would be arriving by the eleven-twenty from London, which got into Salisbury at two o'clock. I looked at my watch. It was eleven thirty-five. The morning bus passing our village went at ten. The afternoon bus left the village at two, and got to Salisbury Market Place at three-seventeen because it detoured through a lot of little places before swinging towards the town. By three-seventeen Mara would have been in Salisbury Station for one hour seventeen minutes, and God knows what she would think of me.

I tried ringing up Salisbury Station to leave a message for her, but they were damn rude to me on the telephone. 'Don't you know there's a war on?' they said. I was in a stew, I felt myself sweating all over, visualizing Mara arriving and finding nobody, and maybe taking the next train back. And then she'd never speak to me again. She'd think I'd let her down.

I dashed into the living room, then to the kitchen. 'Where's Miss Jones?' I asked the Polish girl, meaning Aunt Muriel.

'Miss Jones? She go with Miss Rhoda, in the station-wagon,' she said. 'They come back to lunch.'

That didn't help. I hated Rhoda for doing this to me. And one time she'd said—oh, so many things, about loving me, and wanting me to be happy. I was choking as I thought how beastly it was of Rhoda. I got into my best flannel slacks, my green Braemar twin set, buckled my coat around me. I would have to walk the seven miles to Salisbury. I was a good walker, averaging three miles an hour. With luck, and maybe getting a lift on the way, I could do it.

It was ten minutes past two when I reached Salisbury Station, and I ran into it and started looking for the right platform, which took another three minutes. But when I got there the train hadn't come in yet.

'It's twenty minutes late,' a guard told me, 'Christmas rush.' I never felt more relieved. I sat on a bench opposite the gate of the platform at which the train would arrive, as if looking might make the train come earlier.

And at last it came: the engine, with its round black face like the head of a worm, belching noise and heat and smoke, and then the disgorging sideways of so many people. I was so afraid of missing her. Another gate was opened to let the travellers through more quickly, so with two gates to watch, time and again I thought it was her, and it was not. And suddenly I panicked that perhaps I would not remember her face clearly, and she had slipped past me and was searching for me. Such a flood of people streaming past, and I stared and searched for her face among all those faces.

Then I saw her, and she was not alone. Behind her but obviously attached to her, for she was turning her head to speak to him, was a man in uniform. I stood there, and it was Mara who said: 'Red!' and came to me. She had on a wonderful coat, I thought: deep brown, soft, and a red pixie cap, and of course lipstick, and she looked so utterly different from all the drab, untidy females the war had made of us, it took one's breath away. It was no wonder the officer couldn't stop looking.

'Red,' she said, 'I want you to meet Captain Felton. He very kindly gave me his seat. The train was so full.'

The young man looked pleased. He stared at Mara as if he was going to eat her up, and I thought: he looks like a dog who's going to wag his tail and beg at any moment now. We shook hands, and he said to Mara:

'I'm so sorry I can't give you a lift as I'm going straight on to Bulford in the truck. I'll ring you up, may I, tonight? I might be back in Salisbury in a couple of days. I'd like to show you round, if I may.'

He was all eager beaver, I could see he was quite ready to throw himself at Mara's feet; but she wasn't looking at him, she was looking up in my face, smiling.

She said: 'I'm afraid I'll be busy, I shan't be staying long in Salisbury. I'll be staying with friends.'

She took her suitcase from him. He let go slowly, as if it stuck to his palm. I took the suitcase from her and we walked off. After a few paces I turned. He was still watching her. I felt awkward now, carrying Mara's suitcase. The pleasure of seeing her was over, she was here with me, securely here, and I became cross. Because of that chap, because of Rhoda, because I was very hungry. I had walked seven miles on an empty stomach, and Mara wasn't a bit grateful. She seemed to take my presence there as a matter of course; walked on, swinging her little red handbag and smiling to herself.

'I wonder,' she said, 'if we can get a taxi to the Black Swan? I booked a room there by telephone. You'll stay and have dinner with me, won't you, Red?'

'Considering I haven't had lunch yet, and I must get back to shut up the chickens, I'd better catch the five o'clock bus back.' I added: 'You don't need *me* to look after you.'

'You haven't had lunch?' said Mara. 'Why not?'

'Because, you dumb cluck,' I said, 'if I had had lunch I wouldn't be here now. I've walked seven miles to get here in time. Do you know that? Honestly, I wouldn't do it for anybody else.'

'Oh Red, we must get you something to eat, right away,' she said, 'or you'll faint or something. I do when I don't eat, I pass out.'

'It's all right. I won't pass out.'

But she dragged me to the station buffet and ordered some dried-egg sandwiches, which were pretty grim. I ate some, but there were lots left, and again I felt conspicuous, and irritated with Mara because always something like that would happen when we were together: if it wasn't the bomb it was her husband, or Daphne coming along to have a bath too, or this young chap carrying her suitcase, or people looking at us because she was so different. Always something extra, untoward, out of place. And I hated to be different from other people. I wanted to be approved of, in an unremarkable, unnoticed way. But that could not be with Mara. I couldn't remember how excited I'd been to hear her voice on the telephone yesterday afternoon, how wonderful it had been walking, walking as I had never walked before to get here in time to meet her. Now I resented her, the bondage of love upon me, for I had not learnt that in love there is also bondage, that resentment is always a part of love.

I drank the lukewarm tea, stirred with the spoon tied by a string to the counter, and looked at Mara. Now, because I had eaten and was no longer hungry, I rediscovered her beauty: my irritation went. I wanted to go on sitting in this buffet, looking at her, becoming slowly more and more happy.

59

She said: 'I've been told that the Black Swan is the best hotel in Salisbury, and the food is good, even for wartime.'

'Why didn't you tell me yesterday on the phone that you were coming, Mara, instead of sending a telegram?'

'Because I hadn't decided to come then, I only decided after I'd put the phone down. You'll stay with me, Red, won't you?' she said.

'What about Karl?' I said. Karl had been away when I'd left London.

'Karl may be back tomorrow, so I shall have to return to London tomorrow.'

'It's hardly worth it then,' I said, 'coming just for the day.'

But she said: 'Of course it's worth it.' And I was so happy I could have walked another seven miles there and then. 'Ring up Aunt Muriel,' suggested Mara. 'Tell her you have a friend in Salisbury, and are staying the night.'

Again I felt myself pushed into something I wanted, yet I was afraid to do it because it was upsetting a routine. I liked it, but at the same time I protested: 'I can't, Mara. I can't do this to Aunt Muriel, she'll be hurt.'

'She won't,' said Mara. '*I'll* ring her up. Let's go to the Black Swan.' And of course we did.

They were very nice at the Black Swan. Mara had a way of getting things done simply by looking so sure, and her clothes were always so right. They gave her a lovely double room. We both signed our names. No one seemed to mind at all.

'Now you can stay with me,' said Mara.

I said: 'I hope people won't think things.' I felt more conspicuous than in London: Aunt Muriel was well-known in Salisbury, a lot of people knew me as her niece and heir. But I wanted so much to stay, look at Mara, hold her in my arms again as I had done, feeling whole and peaceful and happy. How much better, I thought, to be in love with Mara than with anyone else, for with Mara until now there had been nothing but this holding of each other and kissing her soft and beautiful mouth, and it seemed quite enough, it seemed all I wanted, for hours and hours. At that time I was pleased that the physical (as I thought) played such a small part in the sum of our feelings, and I thought it would remain like that; and yet, at the same time, already I knew it couldn't.

Mara picked up the telephone and rang Aunt Muriel. Sitting opposite her I could hear Aunt Muriel's voice, and it all seemed so simple and natural that I wondered why I'd been frightened. Mara said she was a friend of mine, passing through Salisbury, and that I'd been good enough to come to the station to meet her and show her round, and could I please stay with her as we had so much to talk about. We were at the Black Swan.

Aunt Muriel was a bit surprised, but she too responded to the upper-class touch in Mara's voice, and of course Mara's voice assured that it would be perfectly all right, and so it was.

Then we were both very happy and hugged each other, and I said, 'Oh, Mara, I missed you so,' even though I had left London only two days before.

Mara had come because of me. Rung up, sent a telegram, come all the way because of me, me, Bettina Jones. Nobody else had done so much for me. Always people had asked me for things, but they'd never *given* me anything; at least, not sought me ou and made me feel like Mara did. I'll never forget it, I thought. This is true love. At that moment I'd have died for Mara.

I helped her unpack, hang her clothes as if she were going to stay for ever, already dreading, as I hung them up, the gesture of tomorrow which would take them down.

* * *

I was braced for a lot of questions from Aunt Muriel when I got back to the farm after breakfast the next day, but the old girl was worried about something else. The Polish cook had had a haemorrhage the night before. It was a threatened abortion. Whether she'd tried to bring it on herself or not, she wouldn't say. I got down to work at once, and Aunt Muriel was so relieved to see me back that she didn't ask any questions.

We ate some cold pie and baked potatoes prepared by Rhoda, and Aunt Muriel said what a blessing Rhoda was. I knew she was a bit peeved at my not being there, because she thought I might have done something to help out. I asked whether the doctor had seen the girl.

'Of course,' said Aunt Muriel sharply, 'Dr Sanders has been. Couldn't let her bleed to death, could we?'

So we didn't talk about my being away, we discussed how to go about getting a substitute, and after lunch Aunt Muriel whisked off with Rhoda in the station-wagon to see some friend of hers in the village who might know of someone to help. But there was a woman-power shortage with the war, and she didn't think anyone could come except old Mrs Wood, seventy-four and a bit, and with rheumatism, possibly just to get lunch going, but no washing up afterwards.

I washed up the dishes alone, then popped upstairs to see the Polish girl. She was looking quite all right, fat and healthy, she had her toddler playing on the bed. In a way I was glad, because with the Polish girl out of action there'd be more to do, and Aunt Muriel probably wouldn't have the heart to ask a lot of questions about Mara. I had a feeling Aunt Muriel might be wiser than she let on; she needed both Rhoda and me to carry on during the Christmas festivities, and somehow I think she might have twigged that Rhoda and I weren't as chummy as before, because she hadn't said things like: 'What've you two been up to now?' when we'd done the chickens or brought the coal in for the furnace together; it was a very small point, but I noticed it: she never used the words 'you two' this time.

The next two days we all had to work hard, the conversation was all on dusting and sweeping and doing the vegs and food, and mash for the chickens, and we were so tired at night that it was easy for me to fall asleep and forget Rhoda in the next bed. Rhoda always got up first while I was still asleep, or pretending to be. And all the time I thought of Mara, and of that night in Salisbury, and the thought was like a flame glowing in me; I ticked off the days on the calendar, wanting to be back in London with Mara.

Aunt Muriel decided to hold the usual Christmas Eve evacuees' tea-party. 'They'd be so disappointed if I didn't.' She was expected to anyway, as chairman of the committee. That meant more work. We rushed round, Mrs Wood came in to help, someone baked buns, I cut the bread and made fish-paste and cheese sandwiches. After lunch Rhoda and I started decorating the room for the tea-party. I pushed the furniture back and removed all the valuable things and put them in Aunt Muriel's own bedroom, just as I'd done the year before. I rolled up the carpets and put them in my bedroom. Aunt Muriel was in the kitchen, the Polish girl had now got up; she hadn't lost the pregnancy after all, and the bleeding had stopped, so she was making trifles with some tinned fruit that had been sent to Aunt Muriel from America for her evacuees. Aunt Muriel wasn't going to ask her who the father was, of course, because that might make her leave; and after all, what with so few men about, and the birth-rate going up anyway, and ATS and WAAFS jumping over the walls at night and tramping miles to Bulford and other men's camps, even Aunt Muriel knew there was such a thing as sex, and not only for cats and dogs and chickens.

Rhoda stood on a step-ladder, winding coloured streamers round the lamp-shades and festooning the walls with the paper chains we'd stored from last Christmas. I didn't know what to do next after pushing the furniture back and rolling up the carpets, and it was awkward asking Rhoda. I thought I'd better start on the Christmas tree, which Rhoda had brought in a few minutes before. So I dragged it in its big flower-pot into the middle of the room, got out the tinsel and glass balls, the stars and the cotton-wool snow, kept in a big box in one of the cupboards in the passage, and I started on the tree.

Then Rhoda came down from the step-ladder, and stood behind me until I had to look at her. She was furious. Her mouth was working, and her hands. 'How dare you,' she said, 'that's my tree. I bought it for Aunt Muriel, don't you dare touch it. I'm going to do it.'

That made me angry. 'Go ahead,' I said, 'I won't touch your bloody tree. In fact, you can do the whole lot from now on, if you like.'

'Oh no you don't,' said Rhoda. 'You stay right here and help, or I'll tell Aunt Muriel.'

'Tell what?' I said. 'My dear Rhoda, aren't you making a prize fool of yourself?'

'I'll tell her about you and that married woman with her painted nails, that Mrs Daniels,' said Rhoda. 'You lied to me. A man, you said.' She spat the word. 'Fancy *you* getting a man. Why, you'll never be able to get a man.'

I said: 'You've no right to talk to me like that.'

'I have every right,' said Rhoda. 'I won't let you get entangled with that woman. She's all painted up and she's older than you, and she's just making use of you, can't you see?'

'So did you,' I said, '*you* also made use of me, and you're also older than me, *much* older.'

She stared at me, dumb with fury. I walked towards her, forcing her to step back. I wanted to hit her, slap her, and in other ways too, hit her with words, make her suffer for all she had done, all the things she had taken from me, the feelings that I'd given fresh and that would never be quite so sincere again.

'You!' I said. 'You, why you've got no right to be in this house! If Aunt Muriel knew the truth about you, you'd be out this very moment on your ear.'

'Red,' she said, 'Red, don't speak to me like that. I love you, and I need you.'

I gave a laugh. 'Tell that to Aunt Muriel,' I said. 'Tell Aunt Muriel how you started on me because I was lonely, how you talked about being a mother to me, remember? And then one night you cried and told me all about the man who'd let you down, remember?'

She leaned against the sofa, sobbing. I hadn't expected her to crumple so quickly.

'Red,' she said, 'Red, please, I didn't use you, I really love you. Why can't we be as we were before? We were so happy.'

'You're ten years older than I am,' I said. 'Ten years. And you've had men. More than one. You've even had a baby and an abortion, or so you told me once, though afterwards you denied it. And it's because that man let you down that you said you hated men and came to me. You started it. You took advantage of me.'

'My God,' said Rhoda, 'you're cruel, aren't you? Well, I can tell you that she'll make use of you too, she's taking advantage of you right now. I bet she's unhappy with her husband, and you're just a filler-in. Because she damn well knows you'll never get a man on your own. She'll throw you away when she's finished with you and has got herself another male. I know her kind. She's a man's woman, she's not your type. She's just fooling around with you between two men, that's all.'

I dug my hands in my pockets. 'That's none of your business, Rhoda. I can take care of myself.'

'All right,' she cried. 'Carry on with that blasted tree. I'm going.'

She rushed out of the room.

I stood for a while with my hands in my pockets, then I took my hands out and started again on the Christmas tree. They were shaking, I hated the shaking and I hated them. Rhoda must have been spying on us, I thought. She must have seen us at the Black Swan, perhaps when Mara and I were having dinner together in the restaurant. 'You'll never get a man, you'll never get a man.' Well, I didn't *want* a man, Mara loved me and she was worth a thousand men.

'You're a beast, Rhoda,' I said out loud.

* * *

The evacuee children's party was rather a strain. I didn't feel I was there, and all this frightful jollity and pretending to enjoy the party games made me sick. In the middle of blind-man's-buff the Polish cook started bleeding again, and Dr Sanders was very annoyed when he came.

'I thought I'd told you she was to stay in bed for a week.' He glared at Aunt Muriel.

Aunt Muriel didn't tell him about the trifles. The Polish girl was weeping out loud and screaming as if she'd die any minute. The kids were kicking each other, somebody's nose bled, so there was human gore all over the place, and Aunt Muriel said she'd never give a party again, it was a waste of time and effort and money. And people were so ungrateful nowadays.

The sight of all this and the noise of children screaming set off something in Rhoda, she sobbed in her pillow that night. I pretended I didn't hear, and after a while she fell asleep.

As I was dozing off I remembered the chickens. I hadn't shut them up, and I bet Rhoda hadn't either. But rather than ask her and hear her snivel, I put on my things and took my torch and went down. Sure enough, nobody had bothered. So that was one more thing I had against Rhoda. It was so cold I shivered all the way back to bed.

Rhoda left the day after Boxing Day, to Aunt Muriel's consternation. She said she'd had an urgent letter from a cousin of hers in Gloucester who wasn't well, and she must go and look after the cousin's children.

'My dear, you're *too* kind,' murmured Aunt Muriel to her, but when she'd left Aunt Muriel said this was most inconsiderate of Rhoda.

'Never heard Rhoda *mention* cousins in Gloucester before,' said Aunt Muriel. I could see her speculating whether Rhoda would be back for the next Christmas holidays. 'Perhaps I'd better find out whether Eunice can come,' said Aunt Muriel, thinking of the chickens. 'She's such a nice girl, so fond of the country, don't you think? I do hope she's got over her conversion by now.'

Eunice was a very distant relation of Aunt Muriel's. She was about twenty-five, and had gone around for years with a girl called Jean. They were so always together that the men students at the Agricultural College all made fun of them. Jean would pull Eunice's hair and scream if she only looked at someone else. Then Eunice became a Roman Catholic. At first Jean didn't seem to mind. But when Eunice became a Child of the Holy Grail League, Jean got quite annoyed. And then Eunice stopped being so much with her, and prayed for her, and Jean became more and more depressed and one day took a heavy dose of sleeping-tablets, and that was that. Eunice now went round with an angelic look and was sweet to everybody. Which is why Aunt Muriel thought of her for the chickens and other chores on the farm.

Then the holidays were over, and there I was with my suitcase packed and some eggs in a carton, pecking Aunt Muriel's cheek and waving goodbye from the train compartment.

When I got to Waterloo I took a taxi from the station and went to Maybury Street. I had written and told Mara I would be back, and the train time, and half expected her at the station. But I knew Karl might be around, and Mara hadn't written to me, or rung up again. But now, Karl or no Karl, I had to go and see her, if only to see the house, to stare at her windows. Then when I was halfway there I got scared that Karl might be there too, and he might think it odd that I'd come with a suitcase. I'd have to leave the suitcase downstairs.

The porter said he didn't know whether Mrs Daniels was in or out, could I go up and try the door? He gave me a haughty nod, and went back to his newspaper. The lift sighed its way up. I stood outside the flat and pressed the bell. I pressed again. Again, and yet once more. No one came.

After a time I went down again in the lift. The streets seemed all changed, empty. My suitcase (the chap looked as if he expected a tip for looking after it) was heavy. I dragged it with me to the corner of the street, and suddenly there she was, walking towards me, and then running, running towards me, and I ran towards her, suitcase and all, and we met; and I could hear her pant and gasp.

'Red, Red, I had to go to the station to see Karl off, and I missed you by about ten minutes.'

We stood looking at each other, laughing, and then I walked

back with her to her flat. Karl had been there most of the holidays, he'd gone just today. That was a blessing. We were very happy about it.

'It's been quite a strain,' she said, and again that pinched look came into her face.

But we didn't want to talk about Karl. That day we decided to have our own place. Mara actually had already arranged it. She'd found a big, clean, double bed-sit in quite a nice house in Bloomsbury, and she said we would share it. Even though it was much better than Nancy's, Mara looked out of place there; but it wasn't too far for her, and she could stay with me when Karl was away and go back to the flat when he was around. It was better than anything else.

The room was pleasant and we had a small kitchenette so that we could cook our own breakfast, or anything else we wanted. Every day Mara went back to her own flat in case Karl had returned – 'Though he always lets me know in advance when he's coming' – to collect the post and the milk, and so that the porter wouldn't become too suspicious. So we managed to be together a lot more.

I bought a little blue notebook for our common expenses, and wrote down our purchases: coffee for breakfast, vegetables, whatever we bought together.

Now I was really happy. I was living with Mara. We never stayed the night at her flat, though I often went there with her in the afternoon after the Horsham and we had baths there. She mussed up the flat a bit too, pretending she'd been sleeping in, and sometimes we'd buy a few things to cook, and eat in her flat before returning home to our bed-sit. Or we'd go to a restaurant, though I was a bit worried about that, although Mara always laughed and said: 'I like to eat something better.' She wouldn't let me share the restaurant bill ever.

Then Karl came back suddenly, without telling her, and luckily it was an afternoon I'd come with her to the flat, and the major-domo downstairs was grinning and said to Mara, 'Mr Daniels is just back, madam, I've just let him in.' So I let her go up alone. And I had a feeling that the chap downstairs knew about us, and it made me very uncomfortable.

I tried not to mind too much. I told myself as soon as Karl left she would be back at night with me, but it was horrid, horrid that night, and the next days and nights. We couldn't speak about it at the Horsham, we pretended there wasn't anything, but we clung fiercely together in our bed-sit, clutching each other, before I let her go, and I saw her to her street corner, as I used to do – but I didn't go to her flat with her, and she didn't ask me. I knew that something would have shown. Then Karl went away again, and we were together once more.

We bought things because it made us feel more together: a second-hand bookcase, which we spent an evening sandpapering and repainting, a coffee-pot in a junk shop, some pictures. Mara brought a wireless because she knew I liked to have it turned on and listen to music or to anything that was going while I was working. She herself didn't like it, and never turned it on of her own accord. Always when we came in, and even before removing my coat, I would walk to the radio and switch it on; but then I always wanted to know what was going on, and Mara never did.

'You don't seem to care a bit about what's going on,' I used to say to her. 'The war might end, and you wouldn't know anything about it.'

'I do care,' said Mara, 'that's why I don't want to know.'

And I loved this in her, it seemed to me then a superiority, something very grand, to care so much she couldn't bear to listen to the radio.

Towards February Daphne started wearing an engagement ring, and simpering that he was a missionary doctor. They'd be going out to work at his mission school and hospital in Africa as soon as the war was over.

'Congrats,' I said, 'hope all your troubles are little ones.'

And she said: 'Oh Red, you're sweet,' but she said it as if I were a boy, and somehow I didn't like it, and going home with Mara that night I was restless.

I turned on the radio, then went to the mirror and looked at myself, Bettina Jones. I was wearing a brown skirt, and I pulled it up to look at my legs.

'You've got very nice legs, Red,' said Mara's voice. She also was in the mirror, behind the leg I extended to look at in profile. I could see her just above my shin bone.

'I'm just wondering what that soppy Daphne's got that I haven't got?'

'Oh Red,' said Mara, 'she's such a soppy little thing, as you say. You're really very beautiful, darling, if only you'd do your hair and get yourself some clothes.'

Mara had already tried getting me some clothes as I had spare coupons, and doing my hair some other way. But I'd always turned round and kissed her and said: 'Not for me, darling, it's you who're the booful one.' But now I looked at myself, came nearer to the mirror to look at eyes, eyebrows, nose, mouth; I rubbed my cheek. My skin had been rather pimply, but since knowing Mara and eating better and being happy, it had become quite good.

Mara came behind me and lifted my hair. 'You ought to cut it,' she said, 'and have a fringe in front, like that. Here, let me show you.'

She twisted it a bit off my face, gathering the bulk behind so I could see the effect.

'You cut it for me,' I said, 'you do yours so well, Mara.'

We twisted a towel round my neck, and she cut away while I watched. I looked different when she'd done it, but it wasn't quite what either of us expected.

'It'd be better if you went to a proper hairdresser,' said Mara.

'It's fine,' I said, and fingered and twisted it. It did look a bit odd.

'Oh Red,' said Mara pitifully, 'I can do mine, but somehow I can't do yours so well.'

'It's lovely,' I said, but I wasn't happy.

The next day she made me go to a hairdresser in Bond Street, and they fixed it and chopped it a bit more, but my face did not look right to me and it cost me a lot of money, twelve shillings.

Then I got some clothes. But in the shops I felt awkward, trying on things. Finally I bought a nice checked dress with a leather belt, but I never wore it much. It was as Mara said: she knew what suited her, but it simply did not look the same on me. And the saleswomen were no help. At Harrods a snooty woman in black brought us things with frills and bows, expensive and reserved, not utility. 'Modom needs something *feminine*,' she said.

'Bitch,' I muttered when her back had turned.

Most of the time we were terribly happy. It seemed to us that what had happened was so different and new, we did not tire of its wonder, we believed that no one else had ever felt the same way, except the poets and they had written just for us. I had no qualms, none of the torturings that had been mine with Rhoda, I was sure this was the real thing at last. I ceased to question the past, and we both dreamed of the future, all we would do together later on. For of that there was little doubt, that Mara and I belonged together, for years and years. That's what we both said.

72

Karl was again back from Europe, but again he came back unannounced, as if he suspected something. Luckily it wasn't at night, it was the evening and Mara hadn't left the flat yet when he turned up. I hadn't gone with her, I'd gone home to get supper ready. I waited and waited for her, and she did not turn up. I rang then, and he answered the telephone, saying: 'Karl Daniels here,' so I muttered: 'Wrong number,' in a muffled voice, and put the telephone down.

Again it was a terrible night, and Mara looked dreadful the next morning. 'I don't think I can go on like that,' she said.

'What did he say?' I asked.

'Nothing, nothing at all,' she said.

But he didn't stay very long, only a few days, then he was gone again. And meanwhile she must have allayed his suspicions, because he told her he wouldn't be back for a month or so. I suspected a trap, but Mara said no, he seemed quite happy. And then she cried a lot at night, but wouldn't tell me why.

It made us both nervous, and sometimes Mara would stay a night in the flat, just on a hunch.

'Wouldn't it be wonderful if we could really get married and live together?' she said.

'Yes,' I said.

We really *felt* married, we felt we belonged together. When Karl was not there.

As March began we took long walks in the evening. We walked along the river, and in Hyde Park. We wandered in the streets in the long-spanned twilight, and one night, pushed by a human flux going the same way, walked to Piccadilly Circus. There, against the walls of the buildings or leaning in the doorways against the closed doors of shops, stood many soldiers, Free French, Poles, but mostly G.I.s. Converging upon them, until each upstanding man was surrounded, lapped like a rock by waves, were women, women of all ages and sizes and descriptions, like a great washing tide, flushing up and down and round and round. And more and more were coming, in that same movement that had pushed us there, until the Circus seemed filled with them, four, five, perhaps more to each man. Mara and I strolled round, circling the Eros which had gone, fascinated and horrified because, not understanding in our own bodies the hunger of others, it appeared strange, alien, abnormal to us, degrading yet gripping in an ugly way which we had escaped, were glad to have escaped. We hovered beyond the lurching groups, went home like cats walking away, superior and free, leaving the milling women and the murmurings and laughter behind us, and did not turn our heads.

On our way home we talked about it, wondering that such things should be, wondering verbally, as people talk who feel detached from their topic.

'I suppose that's what's called normal,' said Mara. 'It's we who are abnormal, Red.'

'I don't know,' I replied. I didn't like the word 'abnormal'.

'I suppose we are what are called lesbians,' said Mara.

'If we are, I suppose we must have been born that way,' I said, 'both of us.'

'I wasn't born that way,' said Mara. 'At least, I don't think so. But now, Red, I don't want to be any way other than I am.'

'Nor me,' I said.

Our little world of trust and tenderness, world enough. Everything and everybody else receded, hazy ghosts in a shadowy play we watched, but nothing they did or said really concerned us. We were happy, and people left us alone.

Mara was convinced that she would never love a man again. 'I thought I was in love with Karl when I married him,' she said.

'But he's horrible, and so are all men. I don't think I would let one touch me again ever.'

We wrapped ourselves closer in our love for each other and felt protected, safe from that other hunger which drove the women to Piccadilly Circus and to the G.I.s. Yet it was when we felt most immune to change that change came.

Until then we had not made love to each other: not in the sense in which two women together enact the ritual gestures of procreation and fulfilment, one the giver, the other the receiver. I don't know why it was so; but there had been always between us restraint and a kind of shyness which was gentle and tender, a deep emotion which kept us from physical exploration. But now we were too much together, the evenings longer, drawn out and restless with lingering, unfinished light. Desire was with us, and Mara was ardent but, I thought, ignorant, and I did not, could not accomplish the realizable if limited caresses that might fulfil her: perhaps my experiences with Rhoda had left a sourness upon me, a too-conscious knowledge I was unwilling to repeat.

I shut my eyes against the erupting past, recollections devoid of meaning now and therefore become ridiculous and obscene. Gestures, strokings, actions which at the time of their performance seemed exalted, even holy; at least exciting and pleasurable. It hurt me to know that some of these gestures and actions I would now repeat with Mara, because although my mind protested that it wasn't the same thing, it wasn't the same at all, yet the deepest part of me knew that sometimes before her mouth, her closed eyes, a taste of Rhoda would come falling upon me, and I was afraid. Even that early, even before we had begun, there was the taint of what had been: the shock of repetition lay between her and me. What I wanted unique bore thus an occasional, hastily crushed resemblance to a memory now rejected. I shook these things away. I firmly shut the door on Rhoda, finishing her off with a final explanation:

'Anyway, Rhoda's a friend of Aunt Muriel's, and she's been staying with us for the hols, but somehow I outgrew her even before I met you. I went off to London and started at the Horsham, and then there was Andy.'

I'd told Mara about Andy because he didn't matter at all, because I didn't want to pretend I didn't know about men.

'But you didn't like Andy, did you? You never did. And you liked Rhoda,' she said one day out of the blue. 'But maybe you'll come to prefer Andy to me in time.'

'Oh, hell no,' I said. 'If there's one thing I know, it's that Andy doesn't mean a thing to me, and never will.'

She slipped by my side, and again I felt protective and protected; we were each other's shelter against all that had been. But this was not to last. In a little while the peace between us was too much for me. I became irritable, angry that at all times our actions and our words fell short of a consummation which we could dream but not perpetrate.

And thus I realized that with Mara it would not be possible for me to pretend to a masculinity which I lacked, certainly not with the artifices which were the lot and the condemnation of such people as we deemed ourselves to be. With Mara, in front of her clear eyes, there could be no such counterfeits or rigmaroles of lust. And her frightened whisper: 'No, no,' stopped me.

One lacerated night when I was frayed and crying: 'For God's sake, oh, for God's sake,' kicking the sheets with frustration, she rose and she whispered: 'Lie down.' And then suddenly it was not the way it had always been, but the reverse, for until now I had always given and as a lover, with hands and mouth and the apings of domination; but now it was not so, it was I who was the woman. I do not know from what innocence or instinct

76

Mara acted, but I know that I was loved and that I knew myself a woman and desirable then. 'Oh Mara,' I said, 'Mara.'

But she would not let me make love to her in the same way. And we were for ever pursued, as all half-hearted things pursue us, with lingering irritation.

But it was a shortcoming so slight, so easily laid by compared with all the rest: the emotional peace, apart from the near but not altogether achieved physical fulfilment; the security and the trust; the sense of caring and being cared for. Tenderness, which made our inadequate loving better than anything we had had so far, made us shrink from desiring more, from desiring too much. These would only be explorations in the physical realms of satisfaction; disgust and satiety would follow, and then we would have doomed ourselves. Therefore we thought we had enough.

*　*　*

Then it was suddenly spring, warm, the 8th of May and VE Day, with an enormous exhilaration which began rather artificially with the radio and the newspapers making it distant instead of near, and suddenly real and intense and joyful when one went out into the mad, shouting streets, with its delirious joys and exuberant displays.

It was with Andy, Andy who had bothered to look me up at the Horsham and knew where I now lived, and a mob of students from St Thomas's and Bart's, that I danced in Piccadilly Circus, blew whistles and cheered buses and sang myself hoarse, and finally got dragged into an all-night pub-crawl and came home with a terrible headache, beating back Andy at the end and locking myself in – Andy, who was saying lots of things about the end of the war, and asking me not to be a spoil-sport and a medieval prig. And the room was empty of Mara, and I threw myself on her bed, breathing in the smell of her hair on her pillow, and cried myself into a drunken sleep.

Mara was not there because Karl was back. She wasn't there that day, or the next, or the next.

The next afternoon Andy came up and apologized, and we had a cup of coffee together. We went to the Everyman to see Anton Walbrook. We had some sandwiches after the film, then I rushed home because I was afraid that Mara might have returned. But she wasn't there, and I was so overwhelmed with loneliness my legs were weak beneath me. Then I went to Nancy's place, and there was Nancy wiping the lino on the table, and the cat walking among the dirty plates and cups and saucers, and Edward with his pipe, and Andy, who gave a shout as he thought I'd come to see him. But I hadn't, I was just lonely for Mara. We sat round and had tea, and Nancy opened a tin of peaches in syrup she'd been hoarding ever since 1942. And later we all had beer, and Nancy got very drunk and began to utter little shrieks as Edward put his hand down her blouse. Soon they'd gone off together. Then somehow Andy was with me in his room, and calling me old thing and using words which were dirty but also exciting in a way; and I was trying to push him away but I had no strength left, and, while he was heaving himself over me and afterwards, my heart kept crying Mara, Mara, Mara, and I didn't feel anything, not a thing.

*　　*　　*

At Mara's return I tried to hurt her as much as her absence had hurt me. When people suffer they take it out on the object of their love, because the object of their love is in their possession. They cannot stop themselves. This goes back to Adam taking it out on Eve, telling God it was her fault; and all our lives we must rend and tear and warp our love to reproduce the primal agony of birth, which is love and hate, joy and suffering, indissoluble together. What I did to Mara then I do to Andy now, but differently because I do not care for him, he only belongs to me. In the ways of wives, I keep him in doubt of himself as a man by making him feel small, by nagging him about his being late for meals, and by rationing him where bed is concerned. Really I don't care at all, but it's a way of passing the time, it affirms the security of my marriage, it is a tug on the chain he wears, re-assuring him too that he is safely imprisoned by me. Mara had hurt me; she had been with Karl for three days. There was no security with her, only the constant fear of losing her, and the bright satin heart of love gets frayed perhaps sooner, shows wear more quickly, than the hempen ropes of marriage.

'Well, stranger?' I said, when she came in breathless on the fourth day, watching the joy wipe itself out, uncertainty creep into the smile on her face; but then she decided that it was affection, I was always a bit abrupt, and she took it as it truly was, a mark of having missed her. Of course it was, but she had no idea how much I would make her pay for having missed her.

She was hugging me when I gave her the second shot: 'Had a good time with Karl?'

'Oh, Red.' She buried her face in my sweater, moving her head against it like a cat rubbing itself, plaintive, placatory. 'Don't let's talk about it, Red. You know it's horrible. I'm back now, that's all that matters.'

But I wouldn't let her push the horror away, I wouldn't give her the tenderness and the peace she wanted, though I could see how thin she was after three days with him, with black shadows under her eyes. Now I can scarcely bring myself to face my own cruelty, it is my punishment, to be borne: how I held her back

79

from me, holding her shoulders, forcing her to look at me, saying: 'What did he do to you *this* time? Tell me' – adding – 'he's a man, isn't he, that precious husband of yours?'

And of course it was horrible because she accepted the cruelty, she wept. She thought she deserved it because I was hurt, she thought I was so hurt in my love for her that I had to hit her with the memories she ran away from. And thus, as Rhoda had done, Mara gave me an excuse for being cruel to her, and it eased my pain to hurt her, it was nearly joy; and after that it became impossible for me to change, to stop hurting her, on and off. It was impossible to go back and acknowledge to her that it was because of what had happened to me the night before, with Andy, that I wanted her to tell me about Karl. I went on pretending it was a kind of pure jealousy, due to my love for her. It was easy, because Mara accepted it at once. She had an essential simplicity where feelings were concerned, too readily she accepted that she was to blame, she could not imagine my double-dealing in my own emotions. If only she'd stopped me then, if only she'd stood up to me ... but she did not. She wept, and tried to console me, though she was the one that was hurt, and even now I marvel that Mara should have been so naive, like a child in her belief that there was never any ulterior motive or intent in what I said and did where she was concerned. She cried, and of course she told me, whispering in my arms, shivering and sobbing great heart-rending sobs, how much she hated Karl, and I felt such a sensation of triumph and of power as I'd never had before.

'I'm going to finish it,' she said. 'You'll see.'

'How?' I said.

'I can't tell you yet, darling, but I'm arranging things, so we can be free, and together, for ever.'

Of course I didn't believe a word of it, it's not easy to get rid of a husband. 'You'll never get rid of Karl,' I said. But I was happy again, in that extraordinary and foolish way in which happiness seems solid, for ever, when it is already rotting in our grasp, when we ourselves have dealt out its death.

It was a couple of days after that, I think (my memory hesitates, perhaps I do not wish to remember), that I gouged out of Mara the recollection of her relationship with Karl.

One thing follows another; the runnels of rainwater bite deeper as they go. It was easy now that Mara had sobbed once to make her sob again, once a week or so. Easy, and queerly satisfying. Some glamour had gone out of my image of her, washed away with her tears. Disappointed that she was vulnerable, that I could make her weep, I made her weep again.

'Tell me,' I said, 'you've got to tell me. I can't go on like that,' putting a desperate, brusque note in my voice, sitting up straight in bed. I didn't feel a thing, yet I did become angry, so that I nearly believed myself when I shook her and said: 'I want to know about Karl and you, d'you hear? I can't bear this kind of thing any more.'

'Oh, Red,' she said (crying, of course), 'you hurt me, Red.'

'And what d'you think you're doing to me?'

I sounded so phoney to myself, how could she not hear it? If she'd turned round, said coldly: 'Don't be silly, Red, stop acting,' I would ... would have been enchanted, ravished with love again, once again her devoted slave, as when she was beautiful and unattainable and wore little gold rings in her ears. She was still beautiful, but she was gentle and tender, and now I was irritated by her beauty. I looked such a wreck when I went out with her, and my hair kept on not being right for my face.

'What d'you think you're doing, trotting up and down whenever Karl returns? How do I know that you don't get on well with him? I've got to know.'

81

And so it came out of her. And now I am ashamed, though when she had finished telling me, I lay back looking into the black night ceiling, coldly: 'Is that all?'

She did not answer, there was only her faint breath, held in long pauses. Soon I was asleep. Perhaps I have the excuse that I did not understand, did not know. To understand one must undergo, and I was not imaginative enough, the capacity to love had been wrung out of me quite early, as it is out of many of us. I slept, and when I woke up next morning I remember I felt pleased and excited, and more cheerful than I had felt for a long time.

Now I can scarcely bear to write this down: boomeranging comes the suffering I did not feel then, alive as it never was. I hope that Mara in time forgot, did not feel this as I do now. I hope she has forgiven me; that in the telling which hurt her she was eased, and did not keep this pain inside her, like a child to be born, through the years as I do.

Some of us are brought up to disfigure love into obscenity. Many of us are twisted to ugliness in thought and deed because we have been made afraid. We do not trust to tenderness any more, and without tenderness towards the other human being little is left but a sad and vicious performance of emotions or contact. Karl, like many others, only knew love, or what he called love, as a domination, an imposition of will, preferably if the imposition was of something slightly tainted and repulsive, like the aroma of high game to bolster appetite. To engender unwillingness, and crush it, and thus enhance authority, that is how we slake our stifled hates. Karl too did this, not because he was evil, but because as with so many of us sex was to him the way out of his weakness; a villainy to be perpetrated like murder, but unlike murder to be got away with unpunished.

Now I understand all this because of Mara, because of Andy.

I go through this embarrassed struggle, quickly done; I too am bent back into myself and can make do with non-feeling, with revenge instead of generosity. So long as the radio is turned on loud I don't have to think about it. I can take it. I can. I think of tomorrow's lunch, and what I'll try to get at Harrods for the kid. And when Andy's done, I hate him calmly and feel superior, and rush off to the bathroom to wash myself clean – clean. And I can think up ways of nagging him so that his manhood will be shorn from him, little by little, so that all that's left of him is a preening body, still pretending to maleness, but getting it over quickly now, getting flabby and coming quickly, and the quicker the better for me. He's really getting impotent; I know, and he knows, but we never talk about it, and I keep an eye on him so he won't stray, and he's scared of me I know. If he'll only do the usual hole-and-corner stuff and if I catch him at it, I'll make him pay for it. Pay and pay. I've got Andy taped.

But Mara couldn't tape anybody. She couldn't let Karl perform his gym exercises and give her mind a wander-off, she couldn't forget about it, or pretend it was all right really. She wanted love to be an open, day thing, clean and tender, not belonging to the murky half-sleep that we all burrow into, eyes shut.

I can give it back to Andy by making him feel he's a louse that's got to be forgiven for doing this. But Mara couldn't give it back to Karl, because she did not know what was to be forgiven. And Karl must have hated her, precisely because she could not giggle when he leered; because she could not provoke rapture by murmuring the dirty words he wanted to hear; and when, in the middle of the honeymoon, drunk for courage to perform on a Mara already shrunk within herself, pitiful and afraid and bewildered, he produced those obscene postcards, bought in Paris, and stuck them round the large bed, and acted them all, one by one, upon her, then she thought she knew that love of man was a beastly thing, the extermination of beauty and tenderness.

'Is that all?' I said.

I do not know what horror I had awaited to thrill me. I was disappointed, and fell asleep. Perhaps Mara, who wanted to be blind because she loved me, told herself that I was trying to alleviate her dread, that out of tenderness and love I had said: 'Is that all?' Why else were we so gay next day? For Mara loved me, I think. What Karl had not valued she tried to give to me. But, alas, I too belonged to that dread company that fills the world, in whom body and mind have been sundered to rage at each other, and love lies to be slobbered over, unextricate from shame.

*   *   *

We laughed a lot that week, nearly a hectic happiness. We went to see a Chaplin revival, *City Lights;* walked in the park, and the ducks with their little round, boot-button eyes made us roar. I talked flippantly about Rhoda, learnedly about the opportunities in a girl's boarding school. We agreed that each human being was both male and female, and anyone who denied both sides in themselves was lying. I analysed myself. 'Expect I was unhappy and lonely – unwanted child, wicked step, all that sort of thing. Then segregation, during the most vulnerable years, exposed to adults who take out their own sexual frustrations upon us youngsters.'

It sounded clever, detached, scientific. A new tranquillity, since I could talk about these things objectively. As if I'd stuck my past in formalin, this scientific approach made it as safe as pieces in a museum.

Mara told me about her family. Mara's father had died when she was young, and all the money had gone to her mother. Her mother was twenty years younger than her father. 'She was just eighteen when she had me, Red, that explains why she's never felt like a mother.' Mara had been brought up mostly in posh boarding schools on the Continent, taken for the holidays to large, rich houses with gay parties and all kinds of idle, rich society people. 'My mother's very gay and beautiful. She's married again, of course, two or three times, but somehow these men never made any difference to her, she's always gay and pretty and having a lovely time and she always has lots of men hanging round. Karl was one of them. I don't really know her well, she's a stranger to me. She's always been very generous. Lots of lovely toys and clothes, but I didn't see much of her. I think that's why I married Karl at nineteen, I wanted to love, to be loved. Karl is rich, but I haven't got anything, not in my own name. Anyway, I've written to my mother (she's in America now, her latest husband is American), told her I want to leave Karl and I want some of my father's money. She's my mother, after all. She's got to help me out.'

And then she said: 'I'm leaving Karl, I'll never go back to him.'

And since Karl was not there, I didn't say anything. I hoped there wouldn't be scenes.

* * *

But it didn't work out that way. One afternoon Mara got a letter from some lawyer in Zürich. The gist of it was that Mara's mother was too busy to write herself, but that she was shocked to hear that Mara was going to leave Karl, she advised strongly against it. She felt that giving Mara any money to help her was unjustifiable in the circumstances. It was all in the kind of language lawyers use, but it was quite plain.

Mara was sitting on the bed, looking at me reading the letter

85

she'd passed to me. 'Well, Red,' she said, 'it doesn't really matter. I'm leaving Karl anyway.'

What could I say? It was so difficult. I loved Mara. Of course. I missed her terribly when she was away. I was sure I loved her. But I didn't know what to say. Of course I wanted her to leave Karl, it was awful when she was with him, but if she left him and there was no money who was going to foot the bills? We went fifty-fifty, except that Mara was extravagant and often bought things to eat and brought them and forgot to enter them in our budget book. I kept the accounts because with Mara we'd never have known how much we spent. There were so many things we did together, and all this I'd have missed so much. But on the other hand, if Mara couldn't get any money from her mother and left Karl flat, then it would be a bit awkward for the bills. I couldn't be expected to foot all the expenses. So I didn't quite know what to say. I said: 'You must do what you think best.'

'Oh, Red, darling,' she said, jumping up and coming to hug me, 'I knew you'd say that. You're so wonderful, really.'

'I'm not.'

'Yes, you are.'

'Look, don't do anything rashly,' I said. 'Think it over carefully. I wouldn't like you to be sorry for whatever you did. I wouldn't want to feel I pushed you into anything.'

She looked at me out of eyes crinkled with happiness.

A few days passed, and nothing happened. She still went back to the flat every day (Karl wasn't there), and now she'd arranged with the chap downstairs to ring her in case he came back unexpectedly. We didn't have a phone in our flat, but there was one in the flat downstairs which belonged to some other people who were obliging and didn't mind an occasional call; in return we got tit-bits for their cat. If ever Karl was to crop up suddenly during the day the chap could ring up either at the College or home. If he came at night then he was to ring, but not after midnight when he was to say that Mara was staying with a friend; in that case he was to ring at seven-thirty in the morning (the people below got up at seven) so she'd be warned.

'But it doesn't really matter now, does it?' said Mara. 'I mean, whether he gets furious or not.'

'What d'you mean, it doesn't matter?'

'Well, I'm going to tell him I don't want to go on with him,' said Mara. 'I've made up my mind, Red. I am not going back to him.'

'Of course. But I wouldn't do anything rash. I mean, don't give the enemy any ammunition, darling. Better have it out quietly.'

She laughed every time I said that. I could see she was gathering up courage for a show-down; but at the same time I knew she wasn't practical, and she might put herself in the wrong, and then it would all be very tricky. Of course it didn't matter if she stayed with me without paying for anything for a few months or so, but it couldn't be for ever, and I didn't know what would happen in the future if she didn't fix things properly. I do hate insecurity and fecklessness, I mean I do want to be able to look a little ahead, and Mara never seemed to look ahead.

Then Aunt Muriel wrote to me that my great-aunt up north had died. 'You know she was a bit strange in her last years,' wrote Aunt Muriel, who had been called to the death-bed. 'Most of the rooms in the house were locked. They were full of trunks and suitcases, all locked too. I had to open them, with the solicitor. They were full of old clothes, old newspapers, pieces of string and tins of food – tins and tins she'd kept, some over twenty years. Your poor aunt was always too careful.'

She'd left thirty thousand pounds, to be divided equally between Aunt Muriel and myself.

'Quite a windfall for you, my dear Bettina, and since you'll be twenty-one soon there won't be any trouble about your getting the money. I'm sure Mr Thurston' – that was Aunt Muriel's lawyer – 'will be only too glad to advise you on the matter of investing it safely and well. He also wishes to tell you about your father's legacy.' I'd have to go up to Thurston's office in Wigmore Street and sign some papers and things, and have the will read to me. In two months' time I would be twenty-one, all the money would come to me: Father's, and my share in my great-aunt's money.

Mara thought I was a bit cut up about my great-aunt because I did suddenly shed a few tears. I was upset, but it was a far-off upset, it wasn't really me getting the letter and crying a bit, it was someone else I could watch doing all this. I told Mara I was getting some money.

'Oh Red, you're an heiress!' said Mara.

'Of course not,' I told her. 'The old girl didn't leave much, and what with death-duties I doubt whether there'll be anything left.'

I went to Mr Thurston's office the next afternoon, and of course Aunt Muriel was already there, in brown tweeds, with a big bag, and a small feather in her hat.

'Well, dear,' said Aunt Muriel after I'd kissed her, 'you do look well. Like your new rooms?'

'They're spiffing,' I said. Aunt Muriel winced, then smiled. I asked about the farm, the chickens, the evacuees. Aunt Muriel was quite happy talking about the farm. The evacuees had gone, but the Polish cook had had her baby and was staying on.

'Bless my soul,' said Aunt Muriel, 'it seems the father may even marry her now. I do hope she'll stay on for a while, though.' I could see Aunt Muriel didn't like the idea of the cook being made into an honest woman and then leaving her.

When Mr Thurston had read the will, and we'd signed papers and things, Aunt Muriel said jocularly: 'Well, it's earlier than expected. How about a cup of tea at your place? I'd love to see it.'

So I had to take her back to our bed-sit, and hope for the best.

'How very cosy,' exclaimed Aunt Muriel, looking at everything. 'You say you are sharing it with … ?'

'Mara Daniels,' I said.

'Ah,' said Aunt Muriel, 'the gal who met you in Salisbury last Christmas?'

'Yes.'

'Is she a widow?' said Aunt Muriel.

'No. I mean, I don't quite know. We don't really ask each other too many questions, you know, Aunt Muriel. She shares this place with me, but of course I don't know much about her. I mean, one doesn't ask questions.' I was floundering a bit, but Aunt Muriel didn't seem to notice.

'Well, I'm sure that's a very good policy,' she said. 'It is *rather* a pity when people get *too* involved with each other, don't you think, dear? Now dear Eunice, such a *nice* girl, but she does get so emotional about people. She's now trying to convert the Polish girl, you know.'

'I thought all Poles were Catholics?'

'This one isn't,' said Aunt Muriel, 'or says she isn't. Dear Eunice is trying to get the man to marry her. I *do* think people ought not to meddle,' said Aunt Muriel, sighing. 'I mean, she might be more unhappy than she is now, don't you think? The baby is perfectly sweet, so good. You must come down at Christmas, and perhaps you can have a chat with Eunice and see whether you can help her a bit. She does get so involved, poor thing.'

She prattled on, and after a time got up and I saw her into a taxi.

I was glad Mara hadn't been in the flat while Aunt Muriel was there. I straightened out the tea things, and when Mara came back I told her about the lawyer, and Aunt Muriel, making it all sound an awful bore.

*   *   *

Then Karl came back. And he came to our flat.

How did he know? At first I thought he must have had Mara watched. It would be quite easy to follow her. But it was simpler.

It must have been about nine-thirty, a warm July twilight. I'd just looked at the clock on the mantelpiece, a rather pretty clock Mara had brought from her flat; I always compared it with my watch to see if it kept time.

There was a ring at the door, and Mara went to open. I wondered who it could be, and somehow (I don't know why) I thought at first it was Andy. At the door stood the outline of a man in a coat with a scarf and no hat. But Mara said: 'Karl –' and Karl came in, and he didn't have his spectacles on.

What a difference that made. Karl without his spectacles had soft, furtive eyes, not like an arrogant human being but something browbeaten; sleepy eyes like a doctored cat. He came in, but didn't look round because he couldn't see, obviously.

'Karl,' she said, and there was a tremor in her voice, 'how … how did you come here?'

'By taxi.' His hand went into his pocket, brought out the frame of his glasses; one of the lenses was cracked and a piece missing. 'Just as I was getting out they fell. I trod on them.' His voice was annoyed. 'The people downstairs guided me here.'

There was quite a silence, and I said: 'Won't you sit down?'

'Thank you,' he said. 'I must say … Mara, what is all this about?' Suddenly he turned towards where she stood, with the oversatined certainty of the half-blind. 'I'm told you're staying here now. Your mother wrote to me that you wanted to leave me. What is all this foolishness?'

'It's true,' said Mara. 'I … I just don't like being married to you, that's all.'

'You don't like being married, that's all. Is there someone else you're interested in, may I ask?'

By his tone of voice I could tell he was quite incredulous. He even looked at me quickly as if to say: isn't this a joke?

'I want to leave you,' said Mara. 'I'd like a divorce, so I can be free.'

Karl turned round to me, laughing. 'I'm sorry this domestic scene has to happen here, Miss … Miss … ?' He'd forgotten my name. Then suddenly he got angry, began to shout, making a kind of grab towards Mara. 'Mara, you cannot do this. You are crazy, crazy. You are a child. I will not let you do this to me, do you hear? You are out of your mind.'

I was up on my feet, but Mara did not understand.

'Bettina,' she said, 'don't.'

Of course I wasn't going to do anything. Just say, if you'll excuse me, and go out. I'd walk about a bit while they were having it out. There was nothing I could do, just standing there.

'Leave us, Bettina,' said Mara.

And I said: 'Righto. I'm going round the corner, got a phone call to make.'

I went down, and on to the street. I did make a phone call, though my hand shook a lot putting the coins in. I called Nancy's place and asked if Andy was there. But he was out.

I walked round for about half an hour, and then suddenly I got terribly frightened. Suppose that man was dragging Mara away,

I'd never see her again. Suppose ... but suddenly I couldn't see him except as a weak man, and I was even sorry for him. I went back and stood outside the door of the flat, but everything was quiet. I opened it and it was dark inside, and I thought for a horrible moment that Mara had gone. But she hadn't, she was just lying down on the bed, flat on her face.

'Well,' I said, 'Karl gone?'

'Yes,' said Mara. 'I've promised to go over to the flat tomorrow and talk it over.'

'Did he ... ?' I began.

'No,' said Mara. 'It never crossed his mind. Another man yes, but not you. I think he was reassured, seeing it was only you.'

So that was all right. 'We'll have to be a bit careful. Karl might turn quite ugly, you know, it would be rather unpleasant.'

'He's got to accept things,' said Mara. 'I'm never going to be his wife again.'

We went to bed on that, but it was some time before I could sleep. I was less frightened, and at the same time something in me smouldered, a burning core of resentment. 'Only you,' Mara had said. Karl hadn't even looked at me as a person. Suddenly I hated them both, Karl and Mara, together.

Then followed days in which Mara wasn't home except late at night. Every day she seemed to be away talking to Karl, and this time I didn't feel too unhappy. We were just beginning our summer vacs, and now the war was nearly over everybody wanted to go somewhere, or spoke of going somewhere for holidays. Mara didn't talk about what Karl was saying to her, and she to him. But when Saturday came round and I was doing the week's expenses, there was no money forthcoming from Mara.

'I couldn't take anything from Karl. Not at this moment.'

'Well,' I said, 'that's O.K. I do understand.'

Another week, and Karl went away. Mara didn't tell me anything much about her talks with Karl, but as the days had gone on she seemed more and more sure of herself. 'He's promised to let me think things over for a couple of months. Karl was worried that it might be another man, and I've told him there isn't one, it's just me, I want to be alone. He asked about you, but I sounded off-hand.'

'He doesn't say anything about me?' I said.

'He seems to take it for granted that you're a friend I'm staying with. I gave our address to my mother. That's how he got to know where I was. She wrote to him. I think,' she said, mouth twisting, 'that Karl and my mother really get on together better than I ever did with either.'

'Nothing doing that side, then,' I said, thinking of the future.

Karl had tried to give her fifty pounds before he left, insisting she take it, but she hadn't and so I was paying for everything now. And then Mara decided we should go for a holiday. Now I want to make it clear that I didn't pick going to Wales. She did. She chose the place, the house and the people. Seeing it now, it looks like too much coincidence that we should have landed just there, but that's how it did happen.

'Peaceful Holiday in beautiful Welsh valley. Excellent food, mod. cons., easy train and transport.' That's what the ad said in *The Times,* and Mara said: 'Let's go there.'

I protested, but she said: 'Oh Red, say yes for a change. And next year,' she added, 'when things are normal again, we'll go round the world.'

'Thanks,' I said, 'I want to get me a job first.'

Mara sent a telegram to the place in Wales, and received a letter back, signed Adelaide Fox, promising home cooking, fresh veg and butter and eggs 'from the farm', and giving directions. We wired the hour of our train arrival, asking for a taxi to meet us. We took the Paddington train, arrived at Carmarthen round three in the afternoon, changed for Llanfolen. Llanfolen turned out to be a minute little station entirely occupied by an enormous, ramshackle Austin, with straw sticking out of its floor, and a man in a peaked cap and a moustache standing next to it looking with strenuous attention at our train.

'You'll be the paying guests for Talybeck Manor, I expect?' the man said to us.

I nodded.

Mara looked at me happily, as if to say: How exciting! She gazed raptly at the Austin.

'Eighteen shillings,' said the man. 'It's a good hour over the hill and into Talybeck. Eighteen shillings you'll owe me for the fare.' He stood there until I had produced the eighteen shillings.

We went over the hill and into a valley, which was Talybeck valley, along a road which wound in lazy long arcs of circle, with woods on one side and deep-folding hills beyond, soft with late afternoon light turning blue. It was a gentle landscape with no bare rock protruding, remote as if withdrawing from contact. I'm not the kind of person who sets out for the Great Unknown and enjoys roughing it without access to the amenities of life, food at the proper time, buses, telephone. As we plunged along the looping road, never meeting any other taxi or car, I became worried thinking how far we had to go; I would have preferred something more accessible, more houses around me, people on the roads. But Mara seemed happy, and I suddenly thought what a bad time she must have had with Karl the last few days, she looked so thin now. But she was full of courage and sureness. And she didn't seem to hate Karl at all now. She spoke quite naturally of him, as if it was already settled. But that was because she already felt free. Marriage has a built-in hypocrisy about it

94

that's so tremendous it keeps the partners together better than love could, but you feel the tension all the time.

So I felt a sudden great love for Mara, and was also sad for both of us. Here we were, carried into an unknown place in a ramshackle taxi – there was something symbolic about it, it was a bit like the future that was coming, so uncertain, and I wanted to put my arms round Mara and say: beloved, tell me that we love each other, tell me not to worry about anything, tell me to be like you, certain and clear and not too practical. But I didn't do it, and the mood wore off, and I became hungry.

The more uncomfortable I was, the bluer and deeper the shades of the woods, the more Mara seemed happy, and finally that happiness without rhyme or reason made me irritable.

The taxi driver unbent and started telling her about Talybeck. 'You'll be staying no doubt with the English ladies who have taken over the Manor,' he said. 'It's a big place.'

'Any other guests?'

'Not that I know of. I haven't taken anybody else this way. The ladies now, they don't know much about the countryside themselves. All these folk down from the cities, they don't find it too easy.'

'I suppose it's the rationing,' I said to the taxi man. 'Where do they shop at Talybeck?'

'Rationing now don't bother us,' said the taxi man. 'There's not much to miss in Talybeck valley. Government doesn't come down here often, so we don't have to bother about rationing. Mind you, it does strike us in the tea, can't have as much tea nor as good quality as before. But you'll be all right anywhere in the valley for food, except for the ladies of Talybeck Manor.'

'Oh?' I said, and glanced at Mara.

'They *buy* their bread, and everything else,' said the taxi man. 'To town they go for it.'

'Oh, look,' cried Mara, 'how beautiful.'

The sun had burst its last slanting gold between two hills, and all the valley glowed. In a few minutes it was gone.

'Did you see, Red, how beautiful that was?'

I said: 'Yes, but we can't live just on sunbeams. I don't like the sound of Talybeck Manor.'

'Then we'll go somewhere else,' said Mara airily.

'But I'll have paid a whole week in advance.' That had been the stipulation, one whole week in advance. 'I wonder if I can get my money back?'

'Oh, Red,' said Mara, 'don't worry about such things now, it's too beautiful to worry.'

The road took a dip, we were on a gravel drive in an unkempt garden, a long drive overshadowed by yews leading to a pile of masonry and brick with window shutters badly in need of paint, and a crowd of children in the most extraordinary, ragged clothes, worse than Aunt Muriel's evacuees, sprawling on the broad steps leading up to the open front door. They now abandoned the steps to gather round the taxi, pushing and shoving each other, and although there were only six of them it looked like a mob. They yelled, too.

'My God,' I said, 'd'you mean to say these kids live here?'

'They're the Talybeck Manor children of the ladies from London,' said the taxi man, clambering out of his machine.

We got out, stood looking at the children, and being stared back at. The oldest couldn't have been more than twelve years old, and the youngest, about three, had his legs in iron calipers.

'Where's your mam?' said the taxi man to the oldest.

'Feeding the baby,' replied the twelve-year-old, and she turned to bawl: 'Ma! Ma!' and all the children took it up. 'Mam! Mam!' they shouted.

'Coming,' said a voice from inside, and with a baby in her

arms out hurried a little brown woman, dark-haired, brown-eyed, with gold rings in her ears, in faded red corduroy slacks with a scarf round her head.

'Oh,' she said, 'you'll be the guests, I expect. Did you have a nice trip down?'

'Quite nice, thank you,' I said.

The little brown woman seemed taken aback. Mara wasn't participating, just looking round with a dreamy look upon her face. The brown woman shifted the baby on to her other arm, and said: 'I expect you'll want to see your room, it's facing the front, so you've got a nice view of the valley.' She said it quickly as if afraid that we might leave on the spot.

'We'd like some tea,' I said, 'if you don't mind. It's rather late.'

'Oh, certainly,' said the little woman, 'I'll get Mrs Fox to make you some tea right away. She's the kitchen department, you know.' She gave a kind of wheezy laugh. 'She's a very good cook. And I suppose you'll want some sandwiches with your tea?'

'Yes,' I said, 'I think we'd like sandwiches, if you have any.'

She gave me another frightened look, and padded away in front of us. Mara and I followed her up a dark staircase to the first floor, and into a large room which didn't look at all bad, with twin beds and a nice high ceiling, a carpet on the floor.

It was true that the view was lovely from here, the valley running before us and the hills seeming to run beside it, like flocks of scampering ponies, and Mara of course would immediately say: 'Oh, how beautiful,' which was quite the wrong thing, because the nut-brown woman said eagerly: 'Yes, it's well worth the trip, isn't it?'

I said: 'We would like our tea fairly soon, please,' just to put her back in her place.

'Oh, yes,' she said, 'and I'll have your luggage sent up immediately.'

'Where's the bathroom?' I asked.

'Oh, the bathroom,' she said. 'Oh, well, we're using the well water at the moment. Something's gone wrong with the pipes. It's only temporary.'

'It said mod. cons. in the advertisement,' I pointed out.

'Oh, Red – ' said Mara.

The little brown woman gave me another of her scared looks, and said: 'Mrs Fox is getting someone from the village to fix the pipes. I expect it will be *quite* all right by tomorrow. Meanwhile, would you like a jug of water sent up?'

'Hot water,' I said, and she gave me another terrified stare and scuttled out, still clutching the baby to her breast.

I was furious. 'Look what you've done,' I said to Mara. 'Got us into this hole, no water, no mod. cons., a battlefield of children including one with infantile paralysis.'

'Red,' said Mara, 'you do look funny when you're bad-tempered.'

'It isn't funny,' I retorted. 'We're going to have a bloody awful time, and it's my only holiday of the year. I don't know what possessed you to pick this place. It's miles from anywhere, and just the train fare cost the earth.'

Then Mara was unhappy too. I had broken her happy mood, and she sat on the edge of one of the twin beds, a bit hunched as if to comfort herself.

I said: 'I suppose we'd better unpack, we can't go anywhere tonight.' I started unpacking.

The tea came, a teapot and a plate of sandwiches, the bread not too well cut and rather stale, but there was lots of milk and sugar, and after tea I felt better.

Then the brown woman brought us two pails of water, luke-warm, and we washed ourselves in the bathroom, which had a tremendous number of rusty pipes protruding from the walls and a lavatory which didn't work. We came back to our room and sat down.

'Thank goodness there's electric light,' said I, turning on the switch.

Later we went to dinner in a downstairs room, the dining-room, which was very beautiful with curved walls and an oval rosewood table to seat about twelve.

The brown woman, who told us her name was Lena Bradford, served us with soup out of a tin, boiled gammon with brussels sprouts and boiled potatoes, not too new, and then a kind of semolina pudding.

'Honestly,' I said to Mara, 'it's exactly the same food as Nancy's, though there are no cat's whiskers here, it's the only difference.'

Then Mrs Fox came in, wiping hands on the apron tied round her middle. She was a short, tough-looking woman, with tough, dry, yellow hair, and she was in slacks. Her eyes flickered from Mara to me, and then back again to Mara, while Lena Bradford hovered around her with little exclamations, saying: 'I was just telling Miss Jones that we were getting a man from the village to come to fix the pipes,' and 'Do let us know what you'd like to have for lunch, we've got masses of eggs, but the vegetables are a bit of a trial ... '

Mrs Fox didn't speak much at all.

We got back to our room and sank into our beds, and, by God, if the sheets weren't damp! Mara looked exhausted.

'It's a hell of a place,' I shouted at Mara. 'It's awful. Why the hell did we come here?'

I heard a sound as if she were giggling, then I found that she wasn't giggling, she was crying; and then I knew what a bitch I'd been to her, and how I'd made everything so ugly, when it was her holiday too. And I came over and soothed her, and my heart burst with remorse, and I stopped saying harsh things to her, and soon she slept, and I lay staring at the ceiling thinking how I'd never do it again, I'd never try to make Mara cry again. Why was I like this to her? After all, we'd decided to stay together, we loved each other. Why then did I do this to her? But, then, why did she cry? Why didn't she stand up and give me back something? She could do it to others. But with me she cried too easily.

*   *   *

We woke to a sun streaming in through the windows, to the howls of children, to a breakfast of three eggs each with bacon, served by the silent Mrs Fox still in the same slacks and sweater. She had a stumpy figure, curiously tight and hard, except for her breasts which sagged the sweater into a flabby oblong from the clavicles to just above the stomach. Her hair looked dyed; from the tangle at the back, straggling loose on her sweater, individual hairs fell upon her back, making me think of Nancy's cat.

Lena came in, holding two children by the hand, and told us the pipes were nearly fixed and now we could use the lavatory flush without having to ladle water out of the pail.

I don't like remembering that morning's discomfort. Mara escaped what I could not, the exacerbation of details of living. But then she had never been really uncomfortable, she wasn't frightened of discomfort because she hadn't really known it. She could soar above it all, be with the sun and with the extending valley, it was all a game to her, and that was intensely aggravating to me. Look here, I wanted to say to her, I've pigged it at Nancy's and elsewhere, not because I had to, but because my step put me to boarding-school early, and I've not known how to enjoy myself, and I certainly don't enjoy paying to be un-

100

comfortable all over again. Like Lenora Stanton with her caravan trips, I can't see any point in being uncomfortable unless you can't afford better. But I couldn't say that, because I could have afforded better than Nancy's place, and I didn't. I didn't because I was scared of spending too much, one never knows what one may need. But I paid quite a bit at Talybeck, and it wasn't worth my money and I felt cheated. That's why I was cross, but I couldn't say all this to Mara, and we both spent the morning pretending everything was all right; but we didn't talk much. Small, trivial things to get upset about – but at the time I felt bruised all over. Mara was all wrong, I didn't like the place, expensive and bad, nor the people, and we would be stuck there for two weeks. It was like being married, for we could not detach ourselves from each other, we couldn't leave each other, we were mentally dragging each other around. Mara was far-away, going away into her own mind for a few minutes at a time, then coming back to me with an effort; we smiled at each other, and made small talk. And we were miserable, yet neither would show it to the other.

Then just before lunch Mara went into the bedroom, re-appeared with crayons and a sketch pad, settled on the porch and began to draw the kids. It was a kind of act she put on: go on, sulk, I don't care, she seemed to say to me. There was about her shoulders and her silence a passive, non-committal acceptance of being buffeted about, but also cutting me out, a tranquil defiance as if she had made herself free of me now, and was absorbed in sketching. I knew those decisions in her, like taking my hand after the bomb and bringing me home, ringing me up on the telephone at Salisbury, coming to Salisbury. But this time it was against me, and it hurt.

And then I began to love her once more, slowly flooded with love of her thin shoulders, her hand with the pencils, her going away from me, and this grew to include the children. But I could not tell her this.

After lunch we walked into the garden and along the gravel drive. It was a bad bit of walking because the gravel was slippery green with mould in places under trees. But as soon as we were out of the gates it was different, open country with sun, and Mara began to loiter, and I fell into her rhythm. We climbed a little hill, walking away from irritation into a vagueness of mind, and I let myself go, unclutching myself (though making a note to remember the way back, Mara couldn't be trusted to remember it and I didn't want to get lost). We walked and Mara led the way though it did not look as if she did, just as if there was a way that she knew, and climbed among pines, and then another hill where we sat on the top among small boulders protruding like bumps under skin, and about us all the hills humped their backs, smooth and round. Everything was clear as far as I could see, except way out on the horizon where there was a little wad of mist like blotting-paper sitting untidily halfway up what looked like higher crests. I looked at my watch to see the time. And then I caught Mara looking at my watch. She'd seen it many times. She never wore a watch. She had an obsession about *not* wanting to know precisely the time.

She said: 'What a nice watch you have, Red. It's just right for you.'

That pleased me. 'Isn't it?' I said. 'Do you know how I got it?'

'No,' she said, 'tell me.'

I told her. My watch is an excellent chronometer watch. I first saw it in the shop window of a jeweller's off the King's Road, a window wedged between two narrow houses. A little Jewish watch-maker sat all day behind this glass pane, little wider than he. The door was very narrow and began immediately where the window left off. The watch had been left in pawn with him by an

American G.I. going to war. One day I looked in the window and saw it. I went in, tried it on and it just fitted my wrist. It would hurt me a lot if I lost it, because it not only gives me the time, but a feeling: the feeling of continuity with the me walking down the King's Road then, with the Jewish watch-maker behind his little glass pane, with the American G.I. leaving the watch for a time as he thought; but it turned out to be for always, the jeweller told me he had been killed in the war.

'It'll go on working for years,' the jeweller had said.

Tick-tick, tick-tick, the watch went on peacefully counting minutes and hours. Security is what I feel as I look at its round placid face, solid, resting on my wrist. It's never gone wrong. The Jewish watch-maker who sold it to me is dead too. We had become friends, and he told me he had an ulcer and I suggested he go to the hospital. I told Andy, and Andy persuaded him to go, so at last he went. They gave him a barium meal and X-rayed him; it wasn't an ulcer, but cancer; they opened him up, and he died.

And Mara now said: 'How terrible,' in a dreamy, drowsy voice, as if it didn't matter. Thinking it over, perhaps that moment was very important – who knows? She didn't show her feelings in the same way as I did. With her everything meant something other than it appeared to me. One couldn't tell. Perhaps she judged me then, judged me and found me wanting.

That afternoon we were happy lying in the sun warming ourselves, being healed in our breach, and I felt I loved her more than ever. Again, as always happens when it is quiet, I was transported back in a tide of remembering. I remembered my mother again. I do this in fits and starts: in Mara's flat the first time I went, a vision of warmth and tenderness which I did not know I possessed until it caught me there; but other visions not so nice, vicious fragments, came back on the Welsh hill. Of the time when my mother ran away from my father with that man (I never could find out whether it was the man at the Zoo or someone else). She took me along, and I saw again the hotel room, with the big double-bed in its middle, so big the room became a three-sided low corridor round it. The smell of damp, similar to the mouldy drive of Talybeck Manor, the soggy grey feel of the sheets, the curtains at the window, badly drawn with a most irritating gap where they wouldn't meet, some kind of brownish-pink material, one corner torn; I remembered my mother wiping my shoes with a corner of the window curtains one afternoon, doing it brusquely, all the time her mouth working, talking angrily with the man whose face I couldn't see even in memory; it had worried me, the ragged edge of the curtain dipping towards the floor, and my mother made the tear worse wiping my shoes. Then I was in a cot with bars; at night, awake, wanting to tell my mother about the curtain, and I stood up in my cot to tell her; but I couldn't see her, only the big bed, the blankets, a big humped mass.

Another memory, another time; perhaps another hotel room, my mother crying, sitting on the edge of another bed, while I stood, holding something, perhaps a doll, staring at her, and then she lifted her skirt and showed me a big bruise, blue-black on her thigh. That man had done it to her. Or was it another man? I remembered again waking up, looking at blankets, looking at the mounds in the bed, like these low hills in Wales, scarcely out of earth. I couldn't see my mother's face at all, nor her hair.

And then, one day, Aunt Muriel in a brown tweed suit and a hat. There had been some shouting and crying, and then I was in a train with Aunt Muriel. I hadn't seen my mother again, and no one mentioned her to me until I was about ten and my step-mother told me she was dead. I'd been at boarding school, and in the holidays back with father in a dim, big house, but he was very busy. I didn't see much of my father, he seemed to travel so much, but I saw quite a lot of my stepmother, she seemed to have appeared suddenly when I was seven or so. I remember her saying to someone one day: 'Of course, the child's mother was low class.' I remember how she tore up in front of me a lot of photographs from a big album that was lying on a top shelf in a wardrobe in a spare room. I knew they were my mother's. I pretended I hadn't seen her do it. Then I wore black back to boarding school; then home again to see my father, terribly ill in bed. I was taken to see him in his bedroom, but I wasn't allowed to stay near him, then one night they woke me up saying: 'Your Daddy wants to see you.'

There was a faint night-light on the table, and his head on the pillow showed two hollows at the temples and two more under the cheek-bones. And suddenly blood began to pour out of his mouth, and my stepmother was sobbing, and I was taken back to bed and I fell asleep.

On the hill in Wales all this came back, but strangely without pain, without this terrible burning inside which made me go out and want to hit somebody. It hurt so little that I could even tell Mara some bits of it, as the memories came. Then Mara gave me her hand, her face was very beautiful, and we walked back again to the house. I thought: now she knows all about me, now she'll know what to do with me. She'll know. She'll know why I am as I am. She'll take me in hand.

* * *

At Talybeck we were miles out of anywhere. Mornings and afternoons we tramped the hills. We went to bed early; I aired the sheets myself. We saw the children, and heard them, but they didn't interfere much with us. Mara sketched the children, and gave the sketches to Mrs Bradford. I thought some of them very good, and told her so, but she said they weren't. I was a bit bored. There was little to read. I listened to the radio in the evenings. Perhaps we really were tired after a hard year at the College, and Karl, and this was right for us.

About the end of the first week Lena Bradford's friendliness became bolder, more pronounced. She lingered after meals trying to talk. She stayed longer and longer with us over coffee, and since there was nothing to do we couldn't push her off. I wasn't anxious to know her or her children, or anything: I didn't want to get involved with anybody. Only a lack of curiosity about others could entrench us in the safety of our mutual world. I felt we must not take on anything or anybody else. People are so damn inquisitive.

But one day, when I'd gone down by myself to the small village about one and a half miles away to fetch some shoes that I'd had re-soled, while Mara was sketching the twelve-year-old, Lena tackled Mara; I found them sitting together on the front-door steps with the children round them. Lena was talking, talking, talking. That is how we got involved with Lena Bradford and Adelaide Fox; not too much, but still emotionally to an extent that wouldn't have happened had I been there that morning and taken Mara away. And once again I ask myself: didn't this, later on, influence us? Is it not partly because of that lovely and wretched holiday that Mara and I did what we did? I keep puzzling over it, but I'll never know.

'Poor Lena,' said Mara to me in our room before lunch, 'she's had an awful time with her husband. He's a terrible man. I'm glad I haven't any children. He just used to make her pregnant all the time, did it to tie her down, to destroy her.'

'That's what *she* says,' I replied.

'But it's true, Red, and she's quite young. She ran away when he tried to make her pregnant again. She says it's jealousy. He's a painter and she wants to write. That's why he's jealous, because she is good at what she does, better than he is. So he found this way to keep her down, married her and gave her lots of children.'

'That sounds a bit like blarney to me,' I answered. 'No woman need have children if she doesn't want them. Perhaps she's a masochist.'

But Mara's sympathy went out to Lena Bradford. 'She's awfully brave,' she said.

'Darling,' I said to her, 'haven't you got enough on your hands with Karl?'

'But that's different,' said Mara. 'I love you and I don't love Karl, and so I have left him. It's all very straightforward.'

'Well, I hope Karl will see it that way. Your mother isn't much help.'

'Oh, Red,' she said, 'nothing matters, so long as I know my own mind. I'm not going back to Karl, come what may.'

Well, there in Wales it sounded obvious, simple and easy. And I thought: of course, even if Karl doesn't give her any money, I've really got enough for both of us, and next year we'll both take jobs or something … I stopped worrying.

The next morning Lena hovered round with more tales of woe; I left Mara for a little while alone and ambled round the garden. The children came round, over-friendly like their mother, with beasties and flowers in their hands. I don't really like children in the mass, but they were so friendly it was difficult to push them away.

That evening both Lena and Adelaide Fox came and sat with us after dinner, after asking us if we'd mind. Of course we had to say we didn't mind. It was a regular session. Lena did most of the talking, and Adelaide Fox sat back and nodded. It developed that Lena thought we might be able to help her by giving witness that her health was ruined, or something to that effect. She thought we were medical students. I suppose this kind of entanglement often happens to doctors, they always get brought into other people's lives; but they know how to disinvolve themselves. But Mara was all for trying to help, perhaps by lending money so that Lena could go and visit a competent doctor, but I said: 'For heaven's sake, don't *you* get into this thing. It won't do any good. She's making quite enough money out of me as it is.'

'Oh Red, but we must help.'

'Why?' I said. 'Am I my brother's keeper? I can't be mixed up with other people's lives, you and I have got our own problems.'

Willy-nilly however we *were* involved. Whenever we met Lena Bradford and Adie Fox, they'd talk about their problem, and their problem was Lena's husband and how he *didn't* provide for his family, and how both of them with the children had to stay here, miles from anywhere, and everything was so difficult because he didn't give his wife any money. Or so they said.

They talked and talked, and Adie analysed Lena's husband too (his name was Henry), described him with the kind of sentences found in psychoanalytical books for the layman: they said he was quite abnormal, and it must be because he'd had such a strict upbringing. Lena hinted at all kinds of things, but somehow it only made me think of Mara, and of myself. Men are odd, there's no doubt about it. They get all kinds of notions. Even Andy. Only I put my foot down; I mean, if I'd let him, he'd just be at it at any old time, even in the kitchen. Lena's talk embarrassed me, and I think it also embarrassed Mara: it brought Karl to her, and it also brought up how I'd made Mara tell me about Karl. And now I feel ashamed of myself, more ashamed of what I'd done than thinking back to what Karl did, because after all men are like that.

Lena said she'd have died of another baby, and she was dead tired, sick of men, she'd never go back to her husband again.

And then a couple of days later, late in the afternoon, a chap with a mac and a fair moustache and his hair all over the place, and lots of battered luggage, arrived in the same taxi we had taken. The children looked at him shyly as he sprang out of the vehicle, and he sort of slobbered over them, saying: 'My dear, dear children,' and grabbed one of them in his arms, and I'm glad to say the kid started howling the place down.

Mara and I stood there looking at the chap going through his father act and saying to the rooted kids: 'Where's your Mum, eh? Let's find your Mum,' looking a bit apprehensively around him, but hugging the kids over and over, calling them 'darlings'. Then he saw us and said: 'Can you tell me where Mrs Bradford is? I'm her husband. My name is Henry Bradford.'

'Come on,' I whispered to Mara, 'let's get out. There's going to be weeping and wailing round here.'

But without waiting for an answer Henry walked round the house, dropping the howling kid. The others ran inside shouting: 'Mam, Mam, Dad's here.'

We went to our room, and I locked the door.

'Damn it,' I said, 'I suppose there will be no dinner cooked tonight.'

We heard voices raised downstairs, and Lena Bradford's loud sobs, and Henry's voice.

'I do hope he doesn't bash her about,' I said. 'I'd hate to be a witness, but if there is any trouble I'll say I didn't hear anything.'

Mara looked at me coldly and said: 'Why are you so afraid of being involved, Red?'

'Because it isn't my business,' I said. 'It's damn stupid, all this, silly people doing silly things. Let them mind their business and I'll mind mine.'

The shouts were getting louder, footsteps came running up the stairs, there was a thumping at our door and Lena shouted: 'Mara, Mara, please open the door and let me in.'

'Don't open,' I said. 'Let them stew in their own juice.'

But of course, like a fool, Mara had already gone to the door and opened it. I had forgotten to put the key in my pocket, I'd left it in the lock.

Lena came hurtling through into our room, and behind her was that man, still in his mac, saying: 'For God's sake listen to me, Lena darling, please!' And then Lena was in Mara's arms, sobbing so loud one couldn't hear oneself speak. The thing that made me most angry was Lena calling Mara by her Christian name, rushing up to her as if they were intimate friends.

Everyone was trying to talk at once, and it ended by me shepherding Lena out and putting her to bed in her bedroom. When I came back to our room there was the chap sitting on my bed talking to Mara.

'It's that woman,' he kept on saying, 'that vicious, pernicious Adelaide Fox. She's a devil. It's she, Mrs Daniels, who's lured my wife from me. I love my wife, I really love her, and my children too, I adore them. They're splendid. She's a splendid wife, and they are wonderful children. There's nothing in the world I wouldn't do for them, and we were so happy, all of us, so happy till that woman came and blasted all my happiness to pieces. She's a wicked woman, Mrs Daniels, wicked and abnormal. We were so sorry for her, Lena and I. Lena took her in, and I never dreamed she'd do this to us. How could I ever dream that my wife, a perfectly normal woman with children and a happy home, would go and fall for that woman's lies? But Lena was like putty in her hands. Of course I knew it was hard on Lena having so many children, and she had always wanted to express herself – she writes *quite* well, you know – but of course I never meant to keep her down, that's a beastly lie. I did all I could to help her, but she herself lost interest in writing. I often asked her: why don't you write any more? And she used to say: "Oh, Henry, haven't got the urge to, these days." Then Mrs Fox came along, and after a while I knew she was plotting against me because Lena refused to sleep with me. She organized a camp-bed for herself. And one night when I came back late I found that she'd moved her bed in with that woman. She'd made up a bed for me in the sitting-room, and they were both in the bedroom. Of course there was a row. Naturally I lost my temper, but I've always loved my wife,' he repeated as an incantation, 'and all I want is for her and my children to come back to me.'

The sap, I thought. What saps men always are, and so incredibly selfish with all their man-made ideas of what women think and how a woman ought to be happy just to be with them. And it isn't quite true, it never is wholly true, women aren't happy just being married and having kids and doing the housework, they want something else too. But we're so unsure of ourselves, we've always been so dependent on their approval, we feel guilty if we're not happy as they tell us we ought to be. How few of us really try to find out what we're like, really, inside?

I didn't like Lena, but I could sympathize with her, hearing that man blab about his Love for her and for his children and how happy their home was. I could picture him making love to her, aah-ing and breathing all over, and she just worried about not getting pregnant and not wanting it, but tired of saying no, and the poor sap couldn't even think of using a cap so's not to get her in trouble; and Lena gradually hating to be touched. I'd get that way with Andy if it wasn't that he is bothering me less and less. But this guy Henry, he must have thought it was like the Holy Sacraments, what he was doing. And now the poor sap started crying, actually crying, and Mara looked unhappy for him and tried to say soothing things.

Henry left our room at last. Mara lay on the bed, face downwards, not looking at me. She had a headache, she told me, and I said no wonder. She put her face in the pillow so that I couldn't see it, and I went out and got some cold water and wrung my handkerchief in it and put it on her forehead.

A little later the oldest girl came to the door to tell us dinner was ready, cold meat and salad, cheese afterwards. Nobody had bothered to cook anything, and it was all on the table. We saw neither Adie nor Lena. There was a hush all over the house, so we went to bed, Mara and I, and lay apart, away from each other, but we spoke about Henry and I told Mara how soppy he was and what I felt about him and Lena. But we didn't discuss Adie. It was difficult going to sleep.

Next morning was a stiff-upper-lip sort of morning, everyone going round holding their feelings in check and being awfully polite. Henry had breakfast with us, then went on with the father act, playing with his children in the garden, wiping their faces with his handkerchief, giving the smaller ones a piggy-back. He must have felt lonely, and suggested we go out for a walk together.

Mara said: 'No thank you, perhaps some other time.'

Then of course he settled down by her, and began to talk of his troubles again. He was at our table again for lunch, sitting at the top of the oval, with Mara on his right and me at his left, and a great big bunch of flowers with sprays of leaves arranged in the middle. He'd picked them early in the morning, he said, and started telling Mara all about the flowers. He felt that he'd added tremendously to the place, picking these flowers, while no doubt Lena and Adie slaved away in the kitchen.

Lena, looking defiant, came in with the soup plates, and Henry sprang up as I'm sure he never had done in his happy home and tried to take the plates from her, and said: 'Please, Lena, won't you sit down?'

And she said: 'Please don't bother.'

He followed her out, and came back later looking like a dog who's been beaten. He was very quiet and ate his soup in audible silence, but he made a heroic effort with the mutton chop and started talking about painting and exhibitions and Continental painters he knew.

'If he's going to be with us at meals from now on,' I said afterwards to Mara, 'we might as well go home right now.'

But there were still three days of our second week to go, and I don't suppose they would have given me back my money, so we might as well stick it out for three more days. And Mara laughed, a bitter little sound, and said: 'We might as well sit it out and see what happens.'

In the afternoon when we came back from a walk for tea, we could hear their voices arguing, this time from the kitchen. There was an awfully oppressive atmosphere. If only we'd kept clear of it from the beginning it would have been much better, we could have ignored the whole thing. Lena and her husband telling us their woes had involved us. We all hung in the same suspense. I blamed Mara for this, though I didn't say anything to her directly. Suddenly on our walk she had begun to be interested in flowers. Since that talk with Henry about painting, and flowers and flowering shrubs on Welsh hills, she looked at the hedges, along the paths, paying attention to what she saw. I wasn't going to hurt Mara any more, even though she picked some leaves and some small flowers and said: 'Yes, that is what he was telling me about,' with a kind of stupid satisfaction, so I didn't say anything. I thought then she was malleable stuff, easily swayed, with not much mind of her own. With terror I thought: why, she's weak, she's influenceable, she doesn't harden herself against things as I do. And for a fleeting panicky moment I thought how easy it would be to lose her. To someone else. A man, for instance. Look at that Henry. The way he spoke to her. If Lena hadn't been around I bet he would have tried, sooner or later. But he never looked at me.

The next morning everything had changed. The first thing was, our breakfast came late, with Adelaide Fox serving us, her hair more in a mess than ever, her face terrible to see, swollen and her lips quivering. Out in the garden Henry and Lena were talking, we could see them through the window.

'They've had a reconciliation,' I said to Mara. 'It's all over now for poor Adie.'

It was pathetic, and yet funny in an uncomfortable way, to see Adie going about looking like death warmed up, not saying a word.

In the afternoon Lena and Henry, like cooing doves, went off with their children, the ideal picture of a Happy Family; they came back with masses of leafage in their arms, and Henry insisted on draping it all over the place.

After tea Henry knocked at our door and came into our room, looking blissful, and started thanking Mara, for what I don't know. Then Lena came in her turn and hugged us both. That night there were more alarums and excursions, with Adie bursting in just as we were going to bed, wearing a purple flannel dressing-gown, with her hair done up in two ridiculous plaits stiffly sticking out from either side of her head behind the ears, her face ploughed up with wrinkles from weeping, and of course she too went straight to Mara and started howling and blubbering.

'He's got her back,' she kept on saying. 'All he had to do was just show himself and she's gone back to him, and what'll he do but give her another kid, and so on till she dies. And she's a much better artist than he is. I know, she's a *real* artist, and he's lousy.'

Poor girl, she looked so awful with that face, those plaits, those sagging breasts.

'I'm sorry,' she said, 'I didn't really want to worry you with all my troubles, but you see how it is.' She gave us a miserable smile-through-tears look. 'You know,' she said, 'if Lena leaves me, I'll just kill myself, that's all. I won't be able to live without her.'

Of course we didn't believe her. There was nothing we could say to her one way or the other, her grief seemed unreal. I was sleepy and couldn't stop yawning, and we were both relieved when she left. That's how tragedy occurs: most of the time it doesn't make one feel anything, it's always more real when it's acted than lived.

The next day at lunch Adie was gone. She must have gone while we were having our usual morning tramp. There was only Lena rushing around looking distrait, laughing a little too much, and Henry smoking a pipe, already installed back in his happy family. He had set up an easel in the garden near the steps, and with a pipe in his mouth, and Lena running round with cups of coffee for him and the children being told to keep quiet, their father was working, everything was coming back to normal.

He told us he would paint the valley. 'Wonderful perspective,' he said.

The next day we went back to London.

It was a few days afterwards that I found it in *The Times,* under the 'Hatches, Matches and Dispatches', which I always read.

FOX. – On August 29th, 1945, suddenly, at York, Adelaide Emily Fox, formerly of Fareham, Hants, dear sister of Charlotte Fox.

There was a paragraph on an inner page about her being found in her room dead from an overdose of sleeping pills. Verdict, accidental death. Her sister vowed she had nothing on her mind at all, was healthy, cheerful, had just taken a job as a nurse-companion to an old gentleman. That's where it had happened. I didn't show the paper to Mara, or tell her about it. I don't think she ever knew.

*　　*　　*

In September we went back to the Horsham for the final year. Karl hadn't given any sign of life for over six weeks, and no money came in, but Mara didn't seem to worry at all.

Poor Lenora Stanton hadn't got through the exams, so she wasn't with us, she was doing second year all over again. She had got married and produced a baby about six months after the wedding. She brought the baby to classes, and when it was feeding time unfolded a screen around herself and said, in that frightfully gay and coy manner of hers: 'Now, now! If you want to look, girls, there's nothing to be ashamed of!' She even fed the baby during Eggie's quiz talks, if they happened to coincide with the baby's feeding schedule, and Eggie couldn't say a thing because Lenora said it was biological and natural. Anyway Eggie suddenly seemed much happier, and then rumours began to go round that she was leaving the Horsham and getting married, which we all said was Incredible. But the rumours persisted.

I had a party for my twenty-first birthday, a small party with Nancy and Andy, both of whom turned up, a couple of other girls, and Mara. I asked Andy to bring another man, and he brought an Egyptian. Andy had scraped through his exams and was now doing a housemanship. Of all things he'd been offered a job in

Singapore, if he got his Tropical Medicine degree in a year's time after that, because his father the bishop had lots of friends there and could pull strings; the salary scale in Singapore was something stupendously high, and he said he longed to find out if it was all true about Eastern girls, so he'd probably go to Singapore. All I knew about Singapore was that the Japs had sunk some of our ships there, and it was on the equator. At the time I was sad to think Andy might go away, but it wouldn't be for another eighteen months, and by then Mara and I would be qualified and have jobs too.

The Egyptian lost his temper over something Nancy said about winning the war, and he said of course the next century would be in Asia and in Africa, and he got awfully excited about colonialism. And Andy said: 'Have a drink, old boy,' and he got even more angry and left soon afterwards.

'I forgot he's a Muslim. They don't drink,' said Andy.

The party was also in the nature of an anniversary for Mara and me, because the year previously we'd met about a week before my birthday, only I hadn't celebrated it that year: just got the usual card from Aunt Muriel and a present from Rhoda, and also a small present from Nancy. But this year I was twenty-one, I was coming into some money of my own, my great-aunt's legacy and my father's, all together about twenty thousand pounds. Of course, I know it sounds like an awful lot of money, but one never knows, and anyway I wasn't going to squander it, but I need not feel so insecure about the future now. Even if Mara didn't get anything from her mother, we might manage; we'd have to be very careful of course, and the sooner there would be jobs for both of us the better. Mara gave me a beautiful hand-painted Italian box, and Aunt Muriel sent some pearls, a pearl necklace which had belonged to her mother and which she'd had restrung for me.

Then a week later of course it all happened, everything came together, like a big wave toppling upon us. I should have realized it would happen, but I didn't, and maybe because everything happened so quickly I panicked and said and did things that finished us. Yet I still believe Mara should have known better, she should have taken things in her hands, as she had done before ... after all, she knew about me. But she didn't do anything, it was left to me.

On Monday afternoon we came back from the Horsham, and I found the letter from Aunt Muriel. When I began to understand what I was reading I had to sit down. Mara was in the kitchen putting the kettle on to boil. When she came back I still had the letter in my hand. I was afraid she might notice, so I went to the W.C. with it and read it again, and then tore it up and flushed it away.

My dear Bettina,

I have been most disturbed by the visit yesterday of a certain Mr Karl Daniels who says he is the husband of your friend. He came unannounced and of course I was quite surprised. He has told me a story which I cannot bring myself to believe to be true. I need not tell you what a shock such a visit is to me at my age, and though it is difficult for me to travel nowadays, as I have had practically no help on the farm and neither you nor Rhoda could manage to come and give a hand this summer, even for a week or so, I shall take the train up to London on Wednesday, the 12.45. I would come earlier, but that I have two committee meetings tomorrow and Tuesday and I must pay a visit to my lawyer. I feel the matter is serious, and I must ask you to meet me at my usual hotel, the Caduceus, for a talk on the matter as soon as you can after your classes that afternoon.

Your affectionate aunt,

MURIEL JONES

'Oh, Christ,' I swore. I went into our bed-sit and drank a cup of tea and tried to look natural. Mara had put her glasses on (she was a little short-sighted) and settled down with a book. I remember it had a blue cover. She looked so placid and calm, she didn't know anything, so I began:

'Well, Mara,' I said, 'the fun's over, I'm afraid.'

She looked up, surprised. 'What is it, Red?' And I saw the quick alarm on her face. She had learnt to be frightened of me. Why should she be scared of me? I was going to pay for all this, wasn't I?

'Your Karl, dear. Your husband. He's gone to Aunt Muriel and poured out a tale of woe. God knows what he's said, but the old girl's coming up the day after tomorrow to have a chat with me. God, what a mess.'

'Was that the letter you were reading?' said Mara, very calmly.

'What do you think?' I hadn't the letter now, I wish I'd kept it to show her. She was so calm, she had no feelings at all. 'The old girl's hopping mad. She'll probably disinherit me now. These things always happen to me,' I said, bitter and flippant. 'Oh, hell.' I stumped away into the kitchen but couldn't do anything there, so came back and threw myself on my bed.

Well, Mara didn't say a word. She just went on reading her book, very calmly. Then we prepared supper. Then we went to bed, saying good night, and she seemed asleep in a moment.

The next day we went to the Horsham as usual. And neither she nor I could speak about Aunt Muriel or Karl. You can say I was unfair, or crafty, or ruthless. You can say what you like.

You can say: why didn't you say anything? What could I say? Mara should have spoken, she should have broken this wall of silence between us. She just did not say a word. And now I feel ... sometimes I feel ... perhaps *she* wanted an opportunity to go away from me, perhaps she had stopped loving me before I stopped loving her.

Then I can't explain my next move, which was to call up Andy during recess hour, and sound sweet and breezy on the telephone, thanking him once again for my birthday present (a little Indian ivory elephant, quite awful really), and he asked me out straight away that evening, as Tuesday happened to be his afternoon and night off till 6 a.m. Maybe I didn't know what I was doing, but I made all the moves, and yet it seemed they just happened. I dressed that evening in a new bronze-coloured dress which suited me (Mara and I had bought it on our return from Wales), I brushed my teeth carefully because when I get too excited sometimes my breath goes bad. I told Mara I'd been asked out by Andy. I said:

'It just slipped my memory. He asked me at my birthday party, as a matter of fact, I forgot to tell you.'

Then all the explaining seemed superfluous because she just nodded, she was reading a book and I noticed it was the same book as yesterday; now I think, I have a feeling, that she didn't turn the pages of that book, just kept it in her hand – but I can't really remember. All this time I never looked at her face, her lovely face, and now I miss it so, and she hasn't left a photograph, not one.

Perhaps I wanted to find Mara gone when I came back that night. I ask myself again, but I no longer know. When I came back late, with Andy kissing and pawing me on the front doorstep, and let myself in, I think I would have howled with misery if she had not been there. But she was there, an immobile and silent lump in bed. She turned when I came in, as if she'd just woken up, and said:

'Had a good time?'

And I said: 'Yes, thanks,' and described the film we'd seen; and we made small talk for a decent interval, then said good night.

All of us double-cross ourselves, pretending, because we can't face all, all the contradictoriness. It makes me laugh now when I hear Andy talking pompously of how concerned he is about the fate of Africans or the spiritual freedom of the Chinese, or one thing or another: because he really doesn't care, it's just a pose, but it makes him feel good that he should have such noble feelings. Well, I'm a double-crosser too, but I feel better because I've owned up to my own other self. While I was breaking up my love for Mara, I could at the same time weep for what I was destroying, and wish it all different; wish myself different from what I was. But of course it could not be.

* * *

There isn't much more to say, but I must put it down.

I went to the Caduceus quite early on Wednesday afternoon. Aunt Muriel was waiting. We chatted about the farm and the Polish cook (she wasn't married yet). Aunt Muriel was wearing her best tweeds, I mean the kind she wears for church, with a grey silk blouse and her amethyst necklace, and that was a bad omen. It meant lawyers and things like family quarrels: she'd worn tweeds to take me away from my mother, and again when once she had a row with my step. It was quite impressive, if I hadn't had something to say I would have been very frightened. There was an awkward silence while Aunt Muriel rang for tea to be served, though it wasn't four yet, but 'they do take ages to serve tea, we might as well ask them slightly earlier,' she said.

Then tea came and we filled up the silences between the chink of china on the tray with questions and answers about my studies, then Aunt Muriel took a deep breath and plunged in:

'I suppose you received my letter, Bettina.'

Obviously I had, since I was here. 'I did, Aunt Muriel.'

Aunt Muriel began to redden slowly. 'I need not tell you,' she said, her voice muffled, 'what a shock, how I felt ... I would like to think the man is mad, Bettina.' She put her cup down. Her hands were shaking. She was obviously very upset.

'Honestly, Aunt Muriel, it's been a shock to me too. Very uncalled for.'

She was breathing a bit better, I must have said that well.

'I'm relieved to hear you say so, Bettina. But this situation must end. It seems to have given rise to considerable misunderstanding, at least in the mind of *one* person. It is really quite thoughtless of Mrs Daniels to leave her home for such long intervals and to stay with you. It might look odd to some people. Very odd. A married woman does not usually leave her home, especially when she is well provided for, to engage in studies, especially prolonged studies. And then to stay with you, to share a residence with another person when she has a perfectly good home of her own ... ' she breathed heavily. 'I told this man that I was convinced there was nothing to it but a very normal friendship. I said you were completely innocent, and probably had never thought of any complications. But you can see, can't you Bettina, what an unpleasant position has arisen? This Mr Daniels seemed quite ready to run to extremes. He is a foreigner, and seems quite highly strung. He even spoke of legal redress, Bettina. I must beg you, for my sake, to stop this friendship of yours at once.'

'But, Auntie, seeing as how I'm engaged to Andy I really don't feel people can misunderstand anything.'

'Don't say "seeing as how", Bettina,' said Aunt Muriel

sharply. 'Really, Bettina, I don't understand how you young people can think it's smart to talk that way. And who's Andy, may I ask? I don't think I know the name.'

I explained about Andrew Morton being the son of a bishop and himself a doctor now doing his housemanship; how I'd known him for years but had waited till I was twenty-one, which was just a week ago. 'Of course, we're not quite officially engaged, Aunt Muriel, because I told him I wanted him to be vetted by you first. But he asked me on my birthday as a matter of fact, and I told him that if ... well, if he came through with you it would be all right with me.'

Aunt Muriel was now so overcome with relief I thought I'd overdone it. She turned purple, then pink, slowly sank back in her chair. Then she gave me a long, long look, and the look went right through me. At that moment I felt sure, absolutely sure, that Aunt Muriel knew everything: I mean, everything about Rhoda, and Mara. I felt she had really always known, but like so many people of her class she was superb at *not* seeing or hearing or knowing things that were unpleasant. And in that flash of intuition I felt nearer to Aunt Muriel than I'd ever been, really close, really of the same flesh and bone, kith and kin. And then I could see her make up her mind that that was the way it was going to be, and she'd decided to see it my way. After all, it was Aunt Muriel who'd come to take me away from my mother, not my own daddy; it was Aunt Muriel who'd fought for me with my step. She knew me through and through.

I wore my best skirt and blouse, and I had her pearls on too, the necklace that she had given me.

'Well,' said Aunt Muriel, 'of course I told the man he was ridiculous, making mountains out of a molehill. But he's a foreigner, that explains his attitude ... they're not very *balanced*, are they? I mean, he was probably rather cruel to his wife and she doesn't like him, and it just happens that you've got yourself involved ... I think you've been rather *careless*, dear. After all, you're an inexperienced young gal, and it never struck you how odd it all *might* look.' Here she took a big gulp: I-may-as-well-say-so sort of thing. 'I didn't really like the idea of this er ... friendship. I blame myself for not saying something about it when I heard she and you were now sharing a ... er ... rooms.' Aunt Muriel couldn't bring herself to say digs.

'Well, Auntie,' I said, 'I can't throw Mrs Daniels out, can I? It's not my fault if she and her husband don't get on, is it?'

Aunt Muriel frowned. 'You could tell Mrs Daniels that I'm very concerned,' she said firmly. 'Meanwhile I could write to this ... to Mr Daniels and tell him that I've had a talk with you and I'm absolutely *convinced* that not only is there nothing to confirm his suspicions, but that should he be so rash as to take certain steps he might find it very difficult ... Of course, it would be most unpleasant, most unpleasant if he did take any legal action, as he threatened to, but he probably wasn't too sure of his ground since he came down to see me first. He said that he had had his wife followed for some time now.' Aunt Muriel's lips curled with dislike. 'At first he thought it was another man, then he found out she was staying with you. Then he gathered that his wife had gone down to visit you in Salisbury last Christmas, then ... well, then he thought it was all very *odd*, especially when his wife said she'd never go back to him. Then you both went off to Wales together. Of course, I'm sure it was quite innocent on your part, but you do see, don't you, what some people might make out of it? Especially in a court of law. I ... actually thought of seeing my lawyer about it, but then I decided I'd see you first ... but you *do* understand that all this must stop at once, don't you? For my sake, Bettina. You must explain the position to Mrs Daniels, and she must leave immediately, or you must.'

Precipitately all was changing, just as if a sudden shrill storm had blown up, obliterating the landscape before me. I was feeling quite sick. Mara, I thought, Mara. What was I doing here? I wanted to shout to Aunt Muriel: 'To hell with Karl, and your money, and everything. I love Mara and she loves me.'

I said: 'I can't ask Mara just to go like that, Aunt Muriel.'

'I'm afraid you'll have to,' said Aunt Muriel sharply. 'I am your guardian, Bettina. You've had a very unhappy start to your life, my dear, and I've always made it a point to look after you to the best of my ability. I don't consider this relationship a healthy one for you. If you do not take steps, I cannot do anything but wash my hands of the whole business since you're now of age. Needless to say I shall consider that I have wasted a good part of my life on someone who does not repay the care and attention I have tried to give, and I shall have to be guided in the future disposal of whatever I may possess by other considerations. I am not saying this as a threat to you, Bettina, but simply because it is the truth. I am an old woman, my dear, and I have had to cope in the past with some very painful situations. I cannot, at my age, be dragged into *another* scandal.'

She's talking of my mother, I thought. It must have been an awful scandal at that time, my mother running away with a man, having lovers, my father divorcing her, my step … My mother low-class, not good enough for my daddy, everyone against her … Aunt Muriel had never mentioned it before. Nobody ever spoke to me of my mother, they'd all kept it from me. But Aunt Muriel must have felt it all these years. It must have been in the newspapers, shame for all to see.

I said: 'I'll try to arrange it, Aunt Muriel, though of course it's difficult when we're both studying.'

Aunt Muriel got up. She pecked me on the forehead, and her eyes were troubled and brimming with tears. I knew she knew

I was lying and I think she did not like me for it. She twisted her amethyst necklace and looked straight into space.

'Bettina, my dear,' she said, 'we all have to do ... certain things. Believe me. I can assure you that ... ' Then she flushed scarlet and her lips tightened. 'Let me know soon ... within a week.'

She wasn't going to let this thing go. She was going to make sure.

So I had to go back, and now it was horrible, horrible; in the bus, like a dim, growling hurricane all round me, my ears filled with the storm wind of what I had done. What had I done, what had I done? What could be done? Mara, Mara, they're trying to break you and me, they're doing this, Mara. Mara, I have to choose. Help me. I was running, running up my street, our street, through thick fog, only there wasn't any fog, but people round me like shadows flitting, turning surprised that I ran, dark against the dark evening, it was so very dark, or so it seemed to me then.

The light was on, the radio too, loud. Mara, Mara, just on the other side of the door. I turned the key, I would see her, I would say: I love you Mara, to hell with Aunt Muriel and the newspapers and the scandal. I love you. Help me. I would see her lovely face.

'Andy, what are you doing here?'

There he was, the slob, spread out on the bed with a conquering hero sort of air, the radio on, just as if he were in his own digs.

'Get your feet off my bed,' I said, 'I won't have filth all over it.' We'd just had the bedspreads laundered, Mara and I. Mara, oh Mara ... a dead hand squeezing me inside, horrible, horrible pain. 'Where's Mara?' I asked.

Andy had got to his feet, looking sheepish and silly, and was sweeping his hand over the bedspread.

'Who?' he said. 'Oh, Mara? She was going out just as I came

up. Met her on the stairs. Fact is, she opened the door for me.'

'Did she say where she was going?'

'Not to me,' said Andy. 'Just said "Bettina won't be long, please come in and sit down." Nice girl,' said Andy. 'Real little woman. Nice shape and hair. Needs a man though, I can see that. Though I prefer the long, lean type ... ' He moved forward, hands foraging; he liked to pinch and tickle, but now I've broken him of that habit.

'Oh, for heaven's sake,' I said.

'C'mon,' he said, 'c'mon, Red, how about some more like last night, eh?' He clucked his tongue. 'Boy, that was good last night.'

Oh God, he was so pleased with himself. Because for once I'd put on a show as if I couldn't resist him any more, as if he was a hell of a guy. All the time I felt like being sick.

'No, thanks. And besides, Mara might come back at any moment.'

'No, thanks,' mimicked Andy. 'Goodness, Red, you say that again and I won't be able to control myself. We'll lock the door.' He winked. 'Won't be long. After all,' he said, 'you might as well get used to it, you know. I'm warning you.' He rolled his eyes again, winking and pinching, irresistible he thought.

'Oh Christ,' I said, 'leave me alone. Not now.'

That made him angry, and he said some nasty things. 'Why, what's the matter? Trying to play me up, or what?' Then he took my hand quick and put it on his trousers, to show me, thinking perhaps that might do it, and started trying to push my skirt up. And now I was scared if I refused he'd back out or something. After all, it hadn't been easy the night before getting him to say: 'I'd marry you if I could, old girl,' and me saying: 'Oh, Andy, but you can,' and artlessly telling him about my twenty thousand pounds. Not shoving it at him, of course, but ... I know what it's like, I know about Andy. The bishop is not well-off, Andy was on a clerical scholarship and always short of money. I knew how he'd react. So I let him, after locking the door, and lay there and thought: God, I'll have to get rid of him, I'm not going to put up with this all my life, night after night. I was so scared Mara would come in I kept my eyes on the door. And the radio played loud, louder, which was good, I'd turned it even higher so I could always say I hadn't heard her knock. Then I got frightened I might not hear her knock – oh, would he never be done? Then I realized something was wrong.

'Hell,' I said, 'what happens if I get pregnant?'

'Eh?' he said. He looked like dropping off to sleep.

But I didn't let him. 'Get up,' I said, 'get out. I don't want Mara to find you here. And I've got to wash. Quick.' I was in a frenzy, and he did go away, thank God, I got him out quick. Then I ran to the bathroom and cleaned myself up, cleaned myself. That would be the worst ever, if I got pregnant.

Then I looked round everywhere, and I felt better, Mara hadn't taken anything, just coat and handbag, everything was here, her dresses, her books, everything. I went to the kitty where we kept the flat money, and there it was, so she couldn't have had any money with her at all, she had no money from Karl. She must have gone for a walk.

I lay down and tried to sleep. I dozed a bit, then I woke up, waiting for her. Then I looked at my watch, dressed and went out, went to the cinema hoping, absurdly, that she might have gone there. It was just closing time, but she wasn't in the crowd coming out. And of course she had no money. I went back and waited. The night went away and Mara did not come back.

It's better now, it will probably get better as time goes on. I know I keep telling myself it's better. I tell myself. I don't seem able to do otherwise than stammer the same words: like the pain that keeps on coming, on and on. At first it was so awful, so terrible, all over again like waking up and seeing the big hump, the colossal mountain of silence and indifference that was my mother and her lover in the bed; night and the face of my father in bed with a driblet of blood between his lips; the little Jew who died of cancer; all, they all came out at me, in and out, all the time, and Mara wasn't there. I cried out for her, oh how I cried out for her. But her face … I could not even get her face back in front of my eyes. Her face is entirely gone from me. And I haven't got a picture of her. Not one. I could say: her nose was straight and small, her eyes were brown, but there is nothing I can take hold of, grasp solidly. Her face is gone from me, as she is gone.

I went to the Horsham. Mara did not come. I waited, every moment thought I could see her. If I just shut my eyes for a moment, then opened them, she'd be there, at my side. But she did not come. The day after there was sunlight coming through the windows, specks of dust dancing in the sunlight, and I wanted to scream: God, her little gold ear-rings. I ran home and ransacked through all her things, her dresses, her extra coat, her books. I found the ear-rings, and kept them in my hand all night: if only I held them in my hand, she might come. She hadn't even taken her pyjamas. Nothing. There was her smell, her perfume, though lately she hadn't been using much; Karl had not brought her any more perfume, and of course I couldn't buy any. For days I lived at night, holding her things in my hands, packing and unpacking them, laying them carefully in the drawers. In the day time I went to the Horsham. Queer, no one came to ask me about Mara. No one mentioned her to me. Not even Louise. One evening, about three days later, the phone rang and I jumped to it, thinking it was Mara, but it was only Andy. I said I was ill with flu.

* * *

129

After nearly a week I couldn't bear it. Mara. I'd written letters to her, left them about the room in case she came back, torn them up in the morning. One night when I was already in bed I got up and put on my slacks and my mac on top (the old mac, the one that I had when I first saw Mara) and I went to Maybury Street. I thought I would ring the bell, and, Karl or no Karl, I'd take Mara away. I would say: 'Come, Mara, come with me. I love you, and neither of us need be frightened of anything because we love each other.' We'd be together, walk together, hand in hand, under the London sky with winter closing in, closing in like a cold tent but the only house we knew. We would be together.

On the way to Maybury Street I suddenly thought: she might be dead, maybe Karl has killed her. I couldn't get my mind off that. Otherwise she would have telephoned, or written. Maybury Street was still some way off, so I hailed a taxi, but when it drew up I couldn't make up my mind, and the driver said: 'Well, I can't wait here all day, lass,' so I said: 'Maybury Street,' and got in.

Maybury Street was awfully quiet, empty. I made him stop past the house. I went walking slowly back, looked up. Her windows were dark. I didn't dare to go in. I stood looking, hoping, willing her to come to a window and look out. Surely, surely, she would hear me, hear me straining to reach her; would wake up, I wanted her so much to wake up and see me. I prayed standing there: 'Oh God, if you are, please make Mara come and look out of the window. No, not even that, just let me see her face, only once more, once more. You see,' I said to God, 'I've forgotten what her face looks like, and that is the worst of all, the worst. Why can't I remember her face? Soon it will all go away from me, like water, like sand washed under one's feet in the tide. I'll have lost all of her, everything, everything of my love, my love … ' And even as I stood there I could feel it going away from me, wearily, weary as an old woman hobbling away. Perhaps I had suffered so much I was worn out and I couldn't feel any more that night.

The next morning I went to see the Secretary at the Horsham, the one who keeps track of our addresses. I said Mara had been unwell for a few days now and had gone down to the country, and did they have her address there? And the Secretary looked at me surprised and said no, they had no news of Mrs Daniels, only the address in Maybury Street. Then she looked concerned and said I must let her know how Mrs Daniels was, if she'd be back soon. I thanked her. And at that moment in came Eggie, and she too was concerned that Mara had missed coming for a week. Eggie had a new suit and looked quite smart. She said:

'Mrs Daniels is *such* an attractive woman, isn't she? I hope she'll get well soon.' Then she looked at me and said: 'You don't look too well yourself?'

Lots of people had colds and flu these days, so I said I wasn't feeling well.

And then on Saturday I got quite a shock, for outside my digs, there on the pavement, stood Karl. He was waiting, looking … just as I must have looked at his flat in Maybury Street. He came striding towards me. I pretended I hadn't seen him, but he could not be avoided.

'Miss Jones,' he said, 'where is Mara?'

'I don't know,' I said.

I kept on walking, but he was at my side, and it wouldn't do, so I stopped. We faced each other. He had his glasses on, they gleamed a bit.

'You don't know,' he said. 'I don't believe it. I'm warning you.'

'It's true. You can have me followed, you can ask anyone. She went away a week ago. I thought she was with you.'

So it had been in vain, waiting in Maybury Street, she wasn't there. And all this time Karl must have been watching me, and realized Mara wasn't with me any more, or he wouldn't have asked. So now we believed each other.

'Where is she?' said Karl. 'Where is she, then?'

'I don't know,' I said.

He turned and left me. I wanted to run after him and say: Look, don't go away, perhaps if we talk a bit we might find her, we might ... But it was too late. He wasn't interested in me at all.

That night I wrote another letter to Mara, upbraiding her for going away. 'Don't you see, darling,' I wrote, 'it was just pretending. I was just pretending to get engaged to Andy, and then you could have gone back to Karl for a bit, but we could still have met each other ... ' Then when I'd written this I realized it wouldn't have worked at all, it could never have been like that. Anyway, Mara had said she wouldn't go back to Karl. She had not gone back. Then where was she?

I've even gone through the 'Dispatches' in *The Times,* all the way back to that day, in case. Nothing. About ten days after she'd gone I made a discovery. I found her key to the Maybury flat and her key to our door. Both together in a small work-basket she had where she kept her thread and needles and things.

*　　*　　*

Well, Andy and I got married in June when I finished at the Horsham. Honeymoon, we went to Belgium, it rained a lot and I was glad to get back. He didn't get his Tropical Medicine degree, so we're staying in England, and he'll have another shot at it in a year or so. Aunt Muriel is talking about a practice in Salisbury for Andy, but what with National Health coming in and the huge pay one gets abroad, Andy says there's a packet to be made in the colonies. And anyway, with my money, and Aunt Muriel's, we can afford to look around a bit before settling down. We've been staying in London, and I haven't done anything much. No point in looking for a job, since I got pregnant on my honeymoon or before. We've got quite a decent flat, plenty of hot water. When Andy isn't there I take walks. I walk and walk around in the streets, and I know what I'm looking for. There are lots of women in the streets, I look at them, sometimes they look back at me. Sometimes one of them looks like Mara, I think it is Mara … but it never is. I even went to Piccadilly Circus several times, in my slacks and old mac: the same as ever, busy, not so many soldiers now, but still lots of women.

Looking for something. Even her name grows faint as an echo at times, at others it's very clear. Perhaps I'll have to go on all my life like this, really searching for her, doing and saying things I don't want to do and to say, always knowing just beyond reach there is something marvellous, unreachable. Well, I am what I am, and did what I did. Who knows, if I'd given up everything for Mara, who knows where we'd be now? Or if it wouldn't have become impossible. Even if there is something else that could have been done or said, it did not happen, it was beyond me to make it happen differently.

And Mara was wrong. She should not have accepted so tamely, have bowed down to my will, or whatever it was that made me do what I did; accepted it and been pushed by it into the night, into going away out of my life, out of life … If she really loved me, she shouldn't have walked out on me. I wake up at night dreaming she is somewhere and I cannot reach her. Sometimes I *wish* she were dead. Then I would stop worrying. She should have been herself with courage, told me what to do. It was she the prime mover, propelling me forward. Why did she give up so easily? Why? Was it because she got tired of loving me? This is what I cannot face: that really she went away because she did not care any more ...

So I write to her, and tear up: rant and rave and tell her that it is her fault, her fault. She should have stopped me. She should not, so easily, have walked out with only her handbag and nothing in it, into the night, disappeared as over the edge of a precipice. I walk the streets looking for her face, like a pearl in the darkness, luminous as I remembered it. And once, coming out of a restaurant, I saw that man, Felton, the chap who had carried her suitcase in Salisbury, talking and laughing with a woman with dark hair down her back. For one crazy moment I was sure it was Mara.

If someone tells me that all my life will be like this, listening to the radio and sleeping and eating with Andy, getting up in the morning and bed at night, I'll kill myself.

Sometimes I pretend that I'm on a hill in Wales, and Mara by my side, the sun dancing on her skin, a little cloud like a blotter on the mountain beyond. I even tried finding those people in Wales, the Bradfords. Perhaps, perhaps, they knew where Mara was. But I couldn't find them.

And so I go on, to go on, as autumn deepens, and darkness draws in to another constricting winter, towards a cold so cold, short days so short you must turn on the lights by four in the afternoon; so I turn on the lights, and the radio loud, and draw the curtains against the night.

Also available in the Lesbian Landmarks series

THE CHILD MANUELA
Christa Winsloe

The novel of the film *Schoolgirls in Uniform*

Manuela von Meinhardis has a loving mother and a callous, egotistical father, an officer in a crack Prussian regiment. On her mother's death Manuela is sent to a repressive school for officers' daughters where all affection is outlawed. The harshness of the regime reflects the iron fist of Prussianism and the Hitlerism already well entrenched by 1932 when Winsloe was writing: the cruelties practised by female staff upon their pupils foreshadow the complicities and horrors of Nazism. In such an environment, only Fräulein von Bernburg offers tenderness and love, and for that both she and Manuela must suffer.

Available in Britain for the first time in more than half a century, *The Child Manuela* is the remarkable and passionate novel on which the famous film *Schoolgirls in Uniform* was based.